F

Also by Brandon Sanderson from Gollancz:

LEGION
SKIN DEEP

BRANDON SANDERSON

Signed by the author

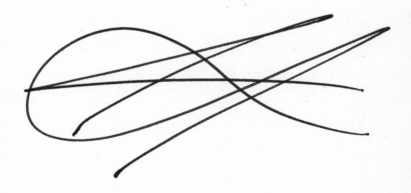

Published by Gollancz
August 2015

LEGION
SKIN DEEP

BRANDON SANDERSON

GOLLANCZ
LONDON

Copyright © Dragonsteel Entertainment, LLC 2014
All rights reserved

The right of Brandon Sanderson to be identified as the author of this
work has been asserted by him in accordance with the
Copyright, Designs and Patents Act 1988.

First published in Great Britain in 2015 by Gollancz
An imprint of the Orion Publishing Group
Carmelite House, 50 Victoria Embankment, London EC4Y 0DZ
An Hachette UK Company

A CIP catalogue record for this book is available
from the British Library

ISBN 978 1 473 21249 7

1 3 5 7 9 10 8 6 4 2

Printed in Great Britain by
Clays Ltd, St Ives plc

The Orion Publishing Group's policy is to use papers
that are natural, renewable and recyclable products and
made from wood grown in sustainable forests. The logging
and manufacturing processes are expected to conform to
the environmental regulations of the country of origin.

www.brandonsanderson.com
www.orionbooks.co.uk
www.gollancz.co.uk

For Greg Creer,
Who was the first person other than myself
to ever read one of my books. Thank you
for the encouragement, my friend!

PART

PART 1

1

'What's her angle?' Ivy asked, walking around the table with her arms folded. Today, she wore her blonde hair in a severe bun, which was stuck through with several dangerous-looking pins.

I tried, unsuccessfully, to ignore her.

'Gold digger, perhaps?' Tobias asked. Dark-skinned and stately, he had pulled a chair over to the table so he could sit beside me. He wore his usual relaxed suit with no tie, and fit in well with this room of crystalline lighting and piano music. 'Many a woman has seen only Stephen's wealth, and not his acumen.'

'She's the daughter of a real estate magnate,' Ivy said with a dismissive wave. 'She has wealth coming out of her nose.' Ivy leaned down beside the table, inspecting my dinner companion. 'A nose, by the way, which seems to have had as much work done on it as her chest.'

I forced out a smile, trying to keep my attention on my dinner companion. I was used to Ivy and Tobias by now. I relied upon them.

But it can be damn hard to enjoy a date when your hallucinations are along.

'So …' said Sylvia, my date. 'Malcom tells me you're some kind of detective?' She gave me a timid smile. Resplendent in diamonds and a tight black dress, Sylvia was an acquaintance of a mutual friend who worried about me far too much. I wondered how much research Sylvia had done on me before agreeing to the blind date.

'A detective?' I said. 'Yes, I suppose you could say that.'

'I just did!' Sylvia replied with a chittering laugh.

Ivy rolled her eyes, refusing the seat Tobias pulled over for her.

'Though honestly,' I said to Sylvia, 'the word "detective" probably gives you the wrong idea. I just help people with very specialized problems.'

'Like Batman!' Sylvia said.

Tobias spat out his lemonade in a spray before him. It spotted the tablecloth, though Sylvia – of course – couldn't see it.

'Not … really like that,' I said.

'I was just being silly,' Sylvia said, taking another drink

of her wine. She'd had a lot of that for a meal that she'd only just begun. 'What kind of problems do you solve? Like, computer problems? Security problems? Logic problems?'

'Yes. All three of those, and then some.'

'That ... doesn't sound very specialized to me,' Sylvia said.

She had a point. 'It's difficult to explain. I'm a specialist, just in lots of areas.'

'Like what?'

'Anything. Depends on the problem.'

'She's hiding things,' Ivy said, arms still folded. 'I'm telling you, Steve. She's got an angle.'

'Everyone does,' I replied.

'What?' Sylvia asked, frowning as a server with a cloth over her arm made our salad plates vanish.

'Nothing,' I said.

Sylvia shifted in her chair, then took another drink. 'You were talking to *them*, weren't you?'

'So you *have* read up on me.'

'A girl has to be careful, you know. There are some real psychos in the world.'

'I assure you,' I said. 'It's all under control. I see things, but I'm completely aware of what is real and what is not.'

'Be careful, Stephen,' Tobias said from my side. 'This is

dangerous territory for a first date. Perhaps a discussion of the architecture instead?'

I realized I'd been tapping my fork against my bread plate, and stopped.

'This building is a Renton McKay design,' Tobias continued in his calm, reassuring way. 'Note the open nature of the room, with the movable fixtures, and geometric designs in ascending patterns. They can rebuild the interior every year or so, creating a restaurant that is half eatery, half art installation.'

'My psychology really isn't that interesting,' I said. 'Not like this building. Did you know that it was built by Renton McKay? He –'

'So you see things,' Sylvia interrupted. 'Like visions?'

I sighed. 'Nothing so grand. I see people who aren't there.'

'Like that guy,' she said. 'In that movie.'

'Sure. Like that. Only he was crazy, and I'm not.'

'Oh, yeah,' Ivy said. 'What a great way to put her at ease. Explain in depth how *not* crazy you are.'

'Aren't you supposed to be a therapist?' I snapped back at her. 'Less sarcasm would be delightful.'

That was a tall order for Ivy. Sarcasm was kind of her native tongue, though she was fluent in 'stern disappointment' and 'light condescension' as well. She was also a good friend. Well, imaginary friend.

She just had a thing about me and women. Ever since Sandra abandoned us, at least.

Sylvia regarded me with a stiff posture, and only then did I realize I'd spoken out loud to Ivy. As Sylvia noticed me looking at her, she plastered on a smile as fake as red dye #6. Inside, I winced. She was quite attractive, despite what Ivy claimed – and no matter how crowded my life had become, it also got terribly lonely.

'So …' Sylvia said, then trailed off. Entrées arrived. She had chic lettuce wraps. I'd chosen a safe-sounding chicken dish. 'So, uh … You were speaking to one of them, just now? An imaginary person?' She obviously considered it polite to ask. Perhaps the proper lady's book of etiquette had a chapter on how to make small talk about a man's psychological disabilities.

'Yes,' I said. 'That was one of them. Ivy.'

'A … lady?'

'A woman,' I said. 'She's only occasionally a lady.'

Ivy snorted. 'Your maturity is stunning, Steve.'

'How many of your personalities are female?' Sylvia asked. She hadn't touched her food yet.

'They aren't personalities,' I said. 'They're separate from me. I don't have dissociative identity disorder. If anything, I'm schizophrenic.'

That is a subject of some debate among psychologists.

Despite my hallucinations, I don't fit the profile for schizo-phrenia. I don't fit *any* of the profiles. But why should that matter? I get along just fine. Mostly.

I smiled at Sylvia, who still hadn't started her food. 'It's not a big deal. My aspects are probably just an effect of a lonely childhood, spent mostly by myself.'

'Good,' Tobias said. 'Now transition the conversation away from your eccentricities and start talking about her.'

'Yes,' Ivy said. 'Find out what she's hiding.'

'Do you have siblings?' I asked.

Sylvia hesitated, then finally picked up her silverware. Never had I been so happy to see a fork move. 'Two sisters,' she said, 'both older. Maria is a consultant for a marketing firm. Georgia lives in the Cayman Islands. She's an attorney …'

I relaxed as she continued. Tobias raised his glass of lemonade to me in congratulations. Disaster avoided.

'You're going to have to talk about it with her even-tually,' Ivy said. 'We aren't exactly something she can ignore.'

'Yes,' I said softly. 'But for now, I'll settle for surviving the first date.'

'What was that?' Sylvia looked at us, hesitating in her narrative.

'Nothing,' I said.

'She was speaking about her father,' Tobias said. 'A banker. Retired.'

'How long was he in banking?' I asked, glad that one of us had been paying attention.

'Forty-eight years! We kept saying he didn't need to continue on ...'

I smiled and began cutting my chicken as she talked.

'Perimeter clear,' a voice said from behind me.

I started, looking over my shoulder. J.C. stood there, wearing a busboy's uniform and carrying a tray of dirty dishes. Lean, tough, and square-jawed, J.C. is a cold-blooded killer. Or so he claims. I think it means he likes to murder amphibians.

He was a hallucination, of course. J.C., the plates he was carrying, the handgun he had holstered inconspicuously under his white server's jacket ... all hallucinations. Despite that, he'd saved my life several times.

That didn't mean I was pleased to see him.

'What are you doing here?' I hissed.

'Watching out for assassins,' J.C. said.

'I'm on a date!'

'Which means you'll be distracted,' J.C. said. 'Perfect time for an assassination.'

'I told you to stay home!'

'Yeah, I know. The assassins would have heard that too.

That's why I had to come.' He nudged me with an elbow. I felt it. He might be imaginary, but he felt perfectly real to me. 'She's a looker, Skinny. Nice work!'

'Half of her is plastic,' Ivy said dryly.

'Same goes for my car,' J.C. said. 'It still looks nice.' He grinned at Ivy, then leaned down to me. 'I don't suppose you could ...' He nodded toward Ivy, then raised his hands to his chest, making a cupping motion.

'J.C.,' Ivy said flatly. 'Did you just try to get Steve to imagine me with a larger chest?'

J.C. shrugged.

'You,' she said, 'are the most loathsome non-being on the planet. Really. You should feel proud. Nobody has imagined anything more slimy, *ever*.'

The two of them had an off-again on-again relationship. Apparently, 'off-again' had started when I wasn't looking. I really had no idea what to make of it – this was the first time two of my aspects had become romantically entangled.

Curiously, J.C. had been completely unable to say the words about me imagining Ivy with a different body shape. He didn't like to confront the fact that he was a hallucination. It made him uncomfortable.

J.C. continued looking the room over. Despite his obvious hangups, he was keen-eyed and very good with security. He'd notice things I would not, so perhaps it was good he'd decided to join us.

'What?' I asked him. 'Is there something wrong?'

'He's just paranoid,' Ivy said. 'Remember when he thought the postman was a terrorist?'

J.C. stopped scanning, his attention focusing sharply on a woman sitting three tables over. Dark-skinned and wearing a nice pantsuit, she turned toward her window as soon as I noticed her. That window reflected back our way, and it was dark outside. She could still be watching.

'I'll check it out,' J.C. said, moving away from our table.

'Stephen ...' Tobias said.

I glanced back at our table and found Sylvia staring at me again, her fork held loosely as if forgotten, her eyes wide.

I forced myself to chuckle. 'Sorry! Got distracted by something.'

'By what?'

'Nothing. You were saying something about your mother –'

'What distracted you?'

'An aspect,' I said, reluctant.

'A hallucination, you mean.'

'Yes. I left him home. He came on his own.'

Sylvia stared intently at her food. 'That's interesting. Tell me more.'

Being polite again. I leaned forward. 'It's not what you think, Sylvia. My aspects are just pieces of me, receptacles for my knowledge. Like … memories that get up and walk around.'

'She's not buying it,' Ivy noted. 'Breathing quickly. Fingers tense … Steve, she knows more about you than you think. She's not acting shocked, but instead like she's been set up on a date with Jack the Ripper and is trying to keep her cool.'

I nodded at the information. 'It's nothing to worry about.' Had I said that already? 'Each of my aspects help me in some way. Ivy is a psychologist. Tobias is a historian. They –'

'What about the one that just arrived?' Sylvia asked, looking up and meeting my eyes. 'The one who came when you weren't expecting?'

'Lie,' Tobias said.

'Lie,' Ivy said. 'Tell her he's a ballet dancer or something.'

'J.C.,' I said instead, 'is ex-Navy SEAL. He helps me with that sort of thing.'

'*That* sort of thing?'

'Security situations. Covert operations. Any time I might be in danger.'

'Does he tell you to kill people?'

'It's not like that. Okay, well, it is *kind* of like that. But he's usually joking.'

Ivy groaned.

Sylvia stood up. 'Excuse me. I need the restroom.'

'Of course.'

Sylvia took her purse and shawl and left.

'Not coming back?' I asked Ivy.

'Are you kidding? You just told her that an invisible man who tells you to kill people just showed up when you didn't want him to.'

'Not one of our smoothest interactions,' Tobias agreed.

Ivy sighed and sat down in Sylvia's seat. 'Better than last time, at least. She lasted … what? Half an hour?'

'Twenty minutes,' Tobias said, glancing at the restaurant's grandfather clock.

'We're going to need to get over this,' I whispered. 'We can't keep going to pieces every time romance is potentially involved.'

'You didn't need to say what you did about J.C.,' Ivy said. 'You could have made something up. Instead, you told her the truth. The frightening, embarrassing, J.C.-filled truth.'

I picked up my drink. Lemonade in a fancy wine glass. I turned it about. 'My life is fake, Ivy. Fake friends. Fake conversations. Often, on Wilson's day off, I don't speak to a single real person. I guess I don't want to start a relationship with lies.'

The three of us sat in silence until J.C. came jogging back, dancing to the side of a real server as they passed one another.

'What?' he asked, glancing at Ivy. 'You chased the chick off already?'

I raised my glass to him.

'Don't be too hard on yourself, Stephen,' Tobias said, resting his hand on my shoulder. 'Sandra is a difficult woman to forget, but the scars will eventually heal.'

'Scars don't heal, Tobias,' I said. 'That's kind of the definition of the word *scar*.' I turned my glass around, looking at the light on the ice.

'Yeah, great, whatever,' J.C. said. 'Emotions and metaphors and stuff. Look, we've got a problem.'

I looked at him.

'The woman we saw earlier?' J.C. said, pointing. 'She –' He cut off. The woman's seat was empty, her meal left half-eaten.

'Time to go?' I asked.

'Yeah,' J.C. said. '*Now.*'

'Zen Rigby,' J.C. said as we rushed from the restaurant. 'Private security – and, in this case, those are fancy words for "killer on retainer". She has a list of suspected hits as long as your psychological profile, Skinny. No proof. She's good.'

'Wait,' Ivy said from my other side. 'You're saying that an assassin really *did* show up at dinner?'

'Apparently,' I replied. J.C. could only know what I did, so if he was saying these things, they were dredged from deep in my memory. I periodically looked over lists of operatives, spies, and professional assassins for missions I did.

'Great,' Ivy said, not looking at J.C. 'He's going to be insufferable to live with now.'

On the way out of the restaurant, at J.C.'s prompting, I looked at the reservation list. That simple glance dumped the information there into my mind, and gave the aspects access to it.

'Carol Westminster,' J.C. said, picking a name off the list. 'She's used that alias before. It was Zen for sure.'

We stopped at the valet stand outside, the rainy evening making cars swish as they drove past on the wet road. The weather dampened the city's normal pungency – so instead of unwashed hobo, it smelled like recently washed hobo. A man asked for our valet ticket, but I ignored him, texting Wilson to bring our car.

'You said she's on retainer, J.C.,' I said as I texted. 'Whom does she work for?'

'Not sure,' J.C. said. 'Last I heard, she was looking for a new home. Zen isn't one of those "hire for a random hit" assassins. Companies bring her on and keep her long-term, use her to clean up messes, fix problems in legally ambiguous ways.'

I knew all of this, deep down, but J.C. had to tell it to me. I'm not crazy, I'm compartmentalized. Unfortunately, my aspects ... well, *they* tend to be a little unhinged. Tobias stood to the side, muttering that Stan – the voice he hears sometimes – hadn't warned him of the rain. Ivy pointedly did not look at the series of small wormholes in the post nearby. Had it always been this bad?

'It could just be a coincidence,' Tobias said to me, shaking his head and turning away from his inspection of the sky. 'Assassins go out for dinner like everyone else.'

'I suppose,' J.C. said. 'If it is a coincidence, though, I'm gonna be annoyed.'

'Looking forward to shooting someone tonight?' Ivy asked.

'Well, yeah, obviously. But that's not it. I hate coincidences. Life is much simpler when you can just assume that everyone is trying to kill you.'

Wilson texted back. *Old friend called. Wanted to speak with you. He is in car. Okay?*

I texted back. *Who?*

Yol Chay.

I frowned. Yol? Was the assassin his? *Fine,* I texted.

A few minutes out, Wilson texted to me.

'Yo,' J.C. said, pointing. 'Scope it.'

Nearby, Sylvia was getting into a car with a man in a suit. Glen, reporter for the *Mag*. He shut the door for Sylvia, glanced at me and shrugged, tipping his antiquated fedora before climbing in the other side of the car.

'I *knew* she had an angle!' Ivy aid. 'It was a setup! I'll bet she was recording the entire date.'

I groaned. The *Mag* was a tabloid of the worst kind – meaning that it published enough truths mixed with its fabrications that people kind of trusted it. For most of my life I'd avoided mainstream media attention, but recently the papers and news websites had latched on to me.

J.C. shook his head in annoyance, then jogged off to scout the perimeter as we waited for the car.

'I *did* warn you something was up,' Ivy said, arms folded as we stood beneath the canopy with the valets, rain pattering above.

'I know.'

'You're normally more suspicious than this. I'm worried that you are developing a blind spot for women.'

'Noted.'

'And J.C. is disobeying you again. Coming on his own when you pointedly left him at home? We haven't ever discussed what happened in Israel.'

'We solved the case. That's all that happened.'

'J.C. shot your gun, Steve. He – an aspect – shot *real people.*'

'He moved my arm,' I said. 'I did the shooting.'

'That's a blurring between us that has never happened before.' She met my eyes. 'You're trying to find Sandra again; I think you purposely sabotaged this date to have an excuse to avoid future ones.'

'You're jumping to conclusions.'

'I'd better be,' Ivy said. 'We had an equilibrium, Steve. Things were working. I don't want to start worrying about aspects vanishing again.'

My limo finally pulled up, Wilson – my butler – driving. It was late evening, and the regular driver only worked a normal eight-hour shift.

'Who's that in the back?' J.C. said, jogging up and trying to get a clear view through the tinted windows.

'Yol Chay,' I said.

'Huh,' J.C. said, rubbing his chin.

'Think he's involved?' I asked.

'I'd bet your life on it.'

Delightful. Well, a meeting with Yol was always interesting, if nothing else. The restaurant valet pulled open the door for me. I moved to step in, but J.C. put his hand on my chest and stopped me, unholstering his sidearm and peering in.

I glanced at Ivy and rolled my eyes, but she wasn't looking at me. Instead, she watched J.C., smiling fondly. What was *up* with those two?

J.C. stood back and nodded, removing his hand from my chest. Yol Chay lounged inside my limo. He wore a pure white suit, a silver bow tie, and a polished set of black-and-white oxford shoes. He topped it all with sunglasses that had diamonds studding the rims – an extremely odd outfit for a fifty-year-old Korean businessman. For Yol, though, this was actually reserved.

'Steve!' he said, holding out a fist to be bumped and speaking with a moderately thick Korean accent. He said the name *Stee-vuh*. 'How are you, you crazy dog?'

'Dumped,' I said, letting my aspects climb in first, so the valet didn't close the door on them. 'The date didn't even last an hour.'

'What? What is wrong with the women these days?'

'I don't know,' I said, climbing in and sitting down as my aspects arranged themselves. 'I guess they want a guy who doesn't remind them of a serial killer.'

'Boring,' Yol said. 'Who wouldn't want to date you? You're a steal! One body, forty people. Infinite variety.'

He didn't quite understand how my aspects worked, but I forgave him that. *I* wasn't always sure how they worked.

I let Yol serve me a cup of lemonade. Helping him with his problem a few years back had been some of the most fun, and least stress, I'd ever encountered on a project. Even if it *had* forced me to learn to play the saxophone.

'How many today?' Yol asked, nodding to the rest of the limo.

'Only three.'

'Is the spook here?'

'I'm *not* CIA,' J.C. said. 'I'm Special Forces, you twit.'

'Is he annoyed to see me?' Yol asked, grinning behind his garish sunglasses.

'You could say that,' I replied.

Yol's grin deepened, then he took out his phone and tapped a few buttons. 'J.C., I just donated ten grand in your name to the Brady Campaign to Prevent Gun Violence. I just thought you'd like to know.'

J.C. growled. Like, *literally* growled.

I leaned back, inspecting Yol as the limo drove us. Another followed behind, filled with Yol's people. Yol had given Wilson instructions, apparently, as this wasn't the way home. 'You play along with my aspects, Yol,' I said. 'Most others don't. Why is that?'

'It's not play to you, is it?' he asked, lounging.

'No.'

'Then it isn't to me either.' His phone chirped the sound of some bird.

'That's actually the call of an eagle,' Tobias said. 'Most people are surprised to hear how they really sound, as the American media uses the call of the red-tailed hawk when showing an eagle. They don't think the eagle sounds regal enough. And so we lie to ourselves about the very identity of our national icon …'

And Yol used this as his ringtone. Interesting. The man answered the phone and began speaking in Korean.

'Do we *have* to deal with this joker?' J.C. said.

'I like him,' Ivy said, sitting beside Yol. 'Besides, you yourself said he was probably involved with that assassin.'

'Yeah, well,' J.C. said. 'We could get the truth out of him. Use the old five-point persuasion method.' He made a fist and pounded it into his other hand.

'You're terrible,' Ivy said.

'What? He's so weird, he'd probably get off on it.'

Yol hung up his phone.

'Any problems?' I asked.

'News of my latest album.'

'Good news?'

Yol shrugged. He had released five music albums. All had flopped spectacularly. When you were worth 1.2 billion from a life of keen commodities investing, a little thing like poor sales on your rap albums was not going to stop you from making more.

'So ...' Yol said. 'I have an issue I might need help with.'

'Finally!' J.C. said. 'This had better not involve trying to make people listen to that awful music of his.' He paused. 'Actually, if we need a new form of torture ...'

'Does this job involve a woman named Zen?' I asked.

'Who?' Yol frowned.

'Professional assassin,' I replied. 'She was watching me at dinner.'

'Could be wanting a date,' Yol said cheerfully.

I raised an eyebrow.

'Our problem,' Yol said, 'might involve some danger, and our rivals are not above hiring such ... individuals. She's not working for me though, I promise you that.'

'This job,' I said. 'Is it interesting?'

Yol grinned. 'I need you to recover a corpse.'

'Oooo ...' J.C. said.

'Hardly worth our time,' Tobias said.

'There's more,' Ivy said, studying Yol's expression.

'What's the hitch?' I asked Yol.

'It's not the corpse that is important,' Yol said, leaning in. 'It's what the corpse knows.'

3

'Innovation Information Incorporated,' J.C. said, reading the sign outside the business campus as we pulled through the guarded gate. 'Even *I* can tell that's a stupid name.' He hesitated a moment. 'It is a stupid name, right?'

'The name is a little obvious,' I replied.

'Founded by engineers,' Yol said, 'run by engineers, and – unfortunately – named by engineers. They're waiting for us inside. Note, Steve, that what I'm asking you to do goes beyond friendship. Deal with this for me, and our debt will be settled, and then some.'

'If a hit woman is really involved, Yol,' I said reluctantly, 'that's not going to be enough. I'm not going to risk my life for a favor.'

'What about wealth?'

'I'm already rich,' I said.

'Not riches, *wealth*. Complete financial independence.'

That gave me pause. It was true; I had money. But my delusions required a lot of space and investment. Many rooms in my mansion, multiple seats on the plane each time I fly, fleets of cars and drivers whenever I wanted to go somewhere for an extended time. Perhaps I could have bought a smaller house and forced my aspects to live in the basement or shacks on the lawn. The problem was that when they were unhappy – when the illusion of it started to break down – things got … bad for me.

I was finally dealing with this thing. Whatever twisted psychology made me tick, I was far more stable now than I had been at the start. I wanted to keep it that way.

'Are you in personal danger?' I asked him.

'I don't know,' Yol said. 'I might be.' He handed me an envelope.

'Money?' I asked.

'Shares in I3,' Yol said. 'I purchased the company six months ago. The things this company is working on are revolutionary. That envelope gives you a ten percent stake. I've already filed the paperwork. It's yours, whether you take the job or not. A consultation fee.'

I fingered the envelope. 'If I don't solve your problem, this will be worthless, eh?'

Yol grinned. 'You got it. But if you do solve it, that

envelope could be worth tens of millions. Maybe hundreds of millions.'

'Damn,' J.C. said.

'Language,' Ivy said, punching him in the shoulder. At this rate, those two were either heading for a full-blown screaming match or a makeout session. I could never tell.

I looked at Tobias, who sat across from me in the limo. He leaned forward, clasping his hands before him, looking me in the eye. 'We could do a lot with that money,' he said. 'We might have the resources, finally, to track *her* down.'

Sandra knew things about me, things about how I thought. She understood aspects. Hell, she'd taught me how they work. She'd captivated me.

And then she'd gone. In an instant.

'The camera,' I said.

'The camera doesn't work,' Tobias said. 'Arnaud said he could be *years* away from figuring it out.'

I fingered the envelope.

'She's actively blocking your efforts to find her, Stephen,' Tobias said. 'You can't deny that. Sandra doesn't want to be found. To get to her, we'll need resources. Freedom to ignore cases for a while, money to overcome roadblocks.'

I glanced at Ivy, who shook her head. She and Tobias disagreed on what we should be doing in regard to Sandra – but she'd had her say earlier.

I looked back at Yol. 'I assume that I have to agree before I can know about the technology you people are involved in?'

Yol spread his hands. 'I trust you, Steve. That money is yours. Go in. Hear them out. That's all I'm asking. You can say yes or no afterward.'

'All right,' I said, pocketing the envelope. 'Let me hear what your people have to say.'

4

I3 was one of those 'new' technology companies, the kind decorated like a daycare, with bright walls painted in primary colors and beanbag chairs set at every intersection. Yol popped some ice cream bars out of a chest freezer and tossed one to each of his bodyguards. I declined, hands behind my back, but he then wagged one at the empty air between us.

'Sure,' Ivy said, holding out her hands.

I pointed, and Yol tossed one in her direction. Which was a problem. Those who work closely with me know to just pantomime, letting my mind fill in the details. Since Yol *actually* threw the thing, my ability to imagine broke down for a moment.

The bar split into two. Ivy caught one, sidestepping the other – the real one – which hit the wall and bounced to the floor.

'I didn't need two,' Ivy said, rolling her eyes. She stepped over the fallen ice cream bar and unwrapped hers, but she looked uncomfortable. Any time a flaw appeared in my ability to mediate between my imaginary world and the real one, we were in dangerous territory.

We went on, passing glass-walled meeting rooms. Most of these were empty, as one would expect at this hour, but every table was covered in small plastic bricks in various states of construction. Apparently at I3, business meetings were supplied with plenty of Legos to accompany the conversation.

'The receptionist at the front desk is new,' Ivy noted. 'She had trouble finding the visitor name badges.'

'Either that,' Tobias said, 'or visitors are rare here.'

'Security is *awful*,' J.C. growled.

I looked at him, frowning. 'The doors are key carded. That's good security.'

J.C. snorted. 'Key cards? Please. Look at all of these windows. The bright colors, the inviting carpets ... and is that a *tire swing*? This place just screams "hold the door for the guy behind you". Key cards are useless. At least most of the computers are facing away from windows.'

I could imagine how this place might feel during the day, with its playful atmosphere, treat bins in the halls and catchy slogans on the walls. It was the sort of environment carefully calculated to make creative types feel comfortable. Like a gorilla enclosure for nerds. The lingering scents in the air spoke of an in-house cafeteria, probably free, to keep the engineers plump and fed – and to keep them on campus. Why go home when you can have a meal here at six? And since you're hanging around, you might as well get some work done …

That sense of playful creativity seemed thin, now. We passed engineers working into the night, but they hunched over their computers. They'd glance at us, then shrink down farther and not look up again. The foosball table and arcade machines stood unused in the lounge. It felt like even in the evening this place should have born a pleasant buzz of chatter. Instead, the only sounds were hushed whispers and the occasional beep from an idle game machine.

Ivy looked to me, and seemed encouraged that I'd noticed all of this. She gestured, indicating that I should go farther. *What does it mean?*

'The engineers know,' I said to Yol. 'There has been a security breach, and they're aware of it. They're worried that the company is in danger.'

'Yeah,' Yol said. 'Word should never have gotten to them.'

'How did it?'

'You know these IT types,' Yol said from behind his sparkling sunglasses. 'Freedom of information, employee involvement, all of that nonsense. The higher-ups held a meeting to explain what had happened, and they invited everyone but the damn cleaning lady.'

'Language,' Ivy said.

'Ivy would like you not to swear,' I said.

'Did I swear?' Yol asked, genuinely confused.

'Ivy has a bit of puritan in her,' I said. 'Yol, what *is* this technology? What do they develop here?'

Yol stopped beside a meeting room – a more secure one, its only glass a small, square window on its door. A handful of men and women waited inside. 'I'll let them tell you,' Yol said as one of his security guards held open the door.

5

'Every cell in your body contains seven hundred and fifty megs of data,' the engineer said. 'For comparison, one of your fingers holds as much information as the *entire internet*. Of course, your information is repeated and redundant, but the fact remains that cells are capable of great storage.'

Garvas, the engineer, was an affable man in a button-down shirt with a pair of aviator sunglasses hanging from the pocket. He wasn't particularly overweight, but had some of the round edges that came from a life working a desk job. He was building a dinosaur out of Legos on the table as he spoke, while Yol paced outside, taking a call.

'Do you have any idea of the potential there?' Garvas continued, snapping on the head. 'As the years pass, technology shrinks, and people grow tired of carrying around bulky laptops, phones, tablets. Our goal is to find a way to do away with that by using the body itself.'

I glanced at my aspects. Ivy and Tobias sat at the table with us. J.C. stood by the door, yawning.

'The human body is an incredibly efficient machine,' said another engineer. A thin man with an eager attitude, Laramie had built his Legos into an ever-growing tower. 'It has great storage, self-replicating cells, and comes with its own power generator. The body is also very long-lived, by current manufacturing standards.'

'So you were turning human bodies,' I said, 'into computers.'

'They're *already* computers,' Garvas said. 'We were simply adding a few new features.'

'Imagine,' said the third engineer – a thin, arrow-faced woman named Loralee. 'Instead of carrying a laptop, what if you made use of the organic computer already built into you? Your thumb becomes storage. Your eyes are the screen. Instead of a bulky battery, you eat an extra sandwich in the morning.'

'That,' J.C. said, 'sounds *freakish*.'

'I'm inclined to agree,' I said.

'What?' Garvas asked.

'Figure of speech,' I said. 'So, your thumb becomes storage. It looks like, what. A … um … USB drive?'

'He was going to say "thumb drive",' Laramie said. 'We really need to stop using thumbs as an example.'

'But it's so *neat*!' Loralee said.

'Regardless,' Garvas said, 'what we were doing didn't change the look of the organ.' He held up his thumb.

'You've had the procedure *done*?' I asked. 'You're testing on yourselves?'

'Freaks,' J.C. said, shifting uncomfortably. 'This is going to be about zombies. I'm calling it now.'

'We've done some very initial tests,' Garvas said. 'Most of what we just told you is just a dream, a goal. Here, we've been working on the storage aspect exclusively, and have made good progress. We can embed information into cells, and it will stay there, reproduced by the body into new cells. My thumb doubles as backup for my laptop. As you can see, there are no adverse effects.'

'We keep it in the DNA of the muscles,' Laramie said, excited. 'Your genetic material has tons of extraneous data anyway. We mimic that – all we have to do is add in a little extra string of information, with marks to tell the body to ignore it. Like commented-out sections of code.'

'I'm sorry,' J.C. said. 'I don't speak super-geek. What did he just say?'

'When you "comment out" something in computer code,' Ivy explained, 'you write lines, but tell the program to ignore them. That way, you can leave messages to other programmers about the code.'

'Yup,' J.C. said. 'Gibberish. Ask him about the zombies.'

'Steve,' Ivy said to me, pointedly ignoring J.C., 'these people are serious and excited. Their eyes light up when they talk, but there are reservations. They are being honest with you, but they *are* afraid.'

'You say this is perfectly safe?' I asked the three.

'Sure,' Garvas said. 'People have been doing this with bacteria for years.'

'The trouble is not the storage,' Loralee said. 'It's access. Sure, we can store all of this in our cells – but writing and reading it is very difficult. We have to inject data to get it in, and have to remove cells to retrieve it.'

'One of our teammates, Panos Maheras, was working on a prototype delivery mechanism involving a virus,' Garvas said. 'The virus infiltrates the cells carrying a payload of genetic data, which it then splices into the DNA.'

'Oh, *lovely*,' Ivy said.

I grimaced.

'It's *perfectly safe*,' Garvas said, a little nervous. 'Panos's virus had fail-safes to prevent it from over-reproducing. We have done only limited trials, and have been very careful. And note, the virus route was only *one* method we were researching.'

'The world will soon change,' Laramie said, excited. 'Eventually, we will be able to write to the genetic hard disk of every human body, using its own hormones to –'

I held up a hand. 'What can the virus you made do *right now?*'

'Worst case?' Loralee asked.

'I'm not here to talk about ponies and flowers.'

'Worst case,' Loralee said, looking to the others, 'the virus that Panos developed could be used to deliver huge chunks of useless data to people's DNA – or it could cut out chunks of their DNA.'

'So … zombies?' J.C. said.

Ivy grimaced. 'Normally, I'd call him an idiot. But … yeah, this kind of sounds like zombies.'

Not again, I thought. 'I hate zombies.'

The engineers all gave me baffled looks.

'… Zombies?' Loralee asked.

'That's where this is going, isn't it?' I asked. 'You turning people into zombies by accident?'

'Wow,' Garvas said. 'That's *way* more awesome than what we actually did.'

The other two looked at him, and he shrugged.

'Mister Leeds,' Laramie said, looking back to me. 'This is not science fiction. Removing chunks of someone's DNA doesn't immediately produce some kind of zombie. It just creates an abnormal cell. One that, in our experiments, has a habit of proliferating uncontrollably.'

'Not zombies,' I said, feeling cold. 'Cancer. You created a virus that gives people cancer.'

Garvas winced. 'Kind of?'

'It was an unintended result that is perfectly manageable,' Laramie said, 'and only dangerous if used malignly. And why would anyone want to do that?'

We all stared at him for a moment.

'Let's shoot him,' J.C. said.

'Thank heavens,' Tobias replied. 'You hadn't suggested we shoot someone in over an hour, J.C. I was beginning to think something was wrong.'

'No, listen,' J.C. said. 'We can shoot Pinhead McWedgy over there, and it will teach everyone in this room an important life lesson. One about not being a stupid mad scientist.'

I sighed, ignoring the aspects. 'You said the virus was developed by a man named Panos? I'll want to talk to him.'

'You can't,' Garvas said. 'He's … kind of dead.'

'How surprising,' Tobias said as Ivy sighed and massaged her forehead.

'What?' I asked, turning to Ivy.

'Yol said a body was involved,' Ivy said. 'And their company is about storing data in human cells, so …'

I looked to Garvas. 'He had it in him, didn't he? The way to create this virus? He stored the data for your product inside his own cells.'

'Yes,' Garvas said. 'And somebody stole the corpse.'

'*Security Nightmare*,' J.C. said as we made our way to the office of Panos, the deceased gene splicer.

'So far as we can tell,' Loralee said, 'Panos's death was perfectly natural. We were all devastated when he had his fall, as he was a friend. But nobody thought it was anything more than a random accident on the ski slopes.'

'Yeah,' J.C. said, walking with my other two aspects just behind him, 'because scientists working on doomsday viruses dying in freak accidents isn't *at all* suspicious.'

'Occasionally, J.C.,' Tobias said, 'accidents *do* happen. If someone wanted his secrets, I suspect killing him and stealing his body would be low on the list of methods.'

'Are you sure he's dead?' I asked Garvas, who walked on my other side. 'It could be some kind of hoax, part of an espionage ploy of some sort.'

'We're very sure,' Garvas replied. 'I saw the corpse. The neck doesn't … uh … turn that way on someone alive.'

'We'll want to corroborate that,' J.C. said. 'Get coroner reports, photos if possible.'

I nodded absently.

'If we follow the simplest line of events,' Ivy said, 'this is quite logical. He dies. Someone discovers that his cells hide information. They snatch the body. I'm not saying it couldn't be something else, but I find what they're saying to be plausible.'

'When did the body disappear?' I asked.

'Yesterday,' Loralee said. 'Which was two days after the accident. The funeral was to be today.'

We stopped in the hallway beside a wall painted with cheerful groups of bubbles, and Garvas used his key card to open the next door.

'Do you have any leads?' I asked him.

'Nothing,' he replied. 'Or, well, too many. Our area of research is a hot one, and lots of biotech companies are involved in the race. Any one of our less scrupulous rivals could be behind the theft.' He pulled open the door for me.

I took the door from Garvas and held it, much to the man's confusion. If I didn't, though, he was likely to walk through while my aspects were trying to enter. The engineers entered. Once they'd gone in, my aspects went through, and I followed. Where had Yol run off to?

'Finding out who did this should be easy,' J.C. said to me. 'We just have to figure out who hired that assassin to watch us. What I don't get is why everyone is so worried. So the nerds accidentally invented a cancer machine. Big deal. I've got one of those already.' J.C. held up a cellphone and wiggled it.

'You have a mobile phone?' Ivy asked, exasperated.

'Sure,' J.C. said. 'Everyone does.'

'And who are you going to call? Santa?'

J.C. stuffed the phone away, drawing his lips to a line. Ivy danced around the fact that none of them were real, but she always seemed – deep down – to be okay with it, unlike J.C. As we walked along this new hallway, Ivy fell in beside him and began saying some calming things, as if embarrassed for calling out his hallucinatory nature.

This newer area of the building was less like a kindergarten, more like a dentist's office, with individual rooms along a hallway decorated in tans with fake plants beside doorways. Garvas fished out another key card as we reached Panos's office.

'Garvas,' I asked, 'why didn't you go to the government with your virus?'

'They'd have just wanted to use it as a weapon.'

'No,' I said, putting my hand on his arm. 'I doubt it. A weapon like this wouldn't serve a tactical purpose in war. Give the enemy troops cancer? It would take months or years to take effect, and even then would be of marginal value. A weapon like this would only be useful as a threat against a civilian population.'

'It's not supposed to be a weapon at all.'

'And gunpowder was first just used to make fireworks,' I said.

'I mentioned that we were looking for other methods to read and write into our cells, right?' Garvas said. 'Ones that didn't use the virus?'

I nodded.

'Let's just say that we started those projects because some of us were concerned about the virus approach. Research on Panos's project was halted as we tried to find a way to do all of this with amino acids.'

'You still should have gone to the government.'

'And what do you think they'd have done?' Garvas asked, looking me right in the eye. 'Pat us on the heads? Thank us? Do you know what happens to laboratories that invent things like this? They vanish. Either they get consumed by the government or they get dismantled. Our research here is important ... and, well, lucrative. We don't want to get shut down; we don't want to be the subject of a huge investigation. We just want this whole problem to go away.'

He pulled open the door and revealed a small, neat office. The walls were decorated with an array of uniformly framed, autographed pictures of science fiction actors.

'Go,' I said to my aspects, holding Garvas back.

The three entered the office, poking and prodding at objects on the desk and walls.

'He was of Greek descent,' Ivy said, inspecting some books on the wall and a set of photos. 'Second-generation, I'd say, but still spoke the language.'

'What?' J.C. said. 'Panos isn't a w–'

'Watch it,' Ivy said.

'– Mexican name?'

'No,' Tobias said. He leaned down beside the desk. 'Stephen, some aid, please?'

I walked over and moved the papers on the desk so Tobias could get a good look at each of them. 'Dues to a local fablab …' Tobias said. 'Brochure for a Linux convention … D.I.Y. magazine … Our friend here was a maker.'

'Speak dumb person, please,' J.C. said.

'It's a subculture of technophiles and creative types, J.C.,' Tobias said. 'A parallel, or perhaps an outgrowth, of the open source software movement. They value hands-on craftsmanship and collaboration, particularly in the creative application of technology.'

'He kept each name badge from conventions he attended,' Ivy said, pointing toward a stack of them. 'And each is signed not by celebrities, but by – I'd guess – people whose talks he attended. I recognize a few of the names.'

'See that rubber wedge on the floor?' J.C. said with a grunt. 'There's a scuff on the carpet. He often stuffed the wedge under his door to prop it open, circumventing the auto-lock. He liked to leave his office open for people to stop by and chat.'

I poked at a few stickers stuck to the top of his desk. *Support Open Source, Information for Every Body, Words Should Be Free.*

Tobias had me sit at the computer. It wasn't password protected. J.C. raised an eyebrow.

Panos's latest website visits were forums, where he posted energetically, but politely, about information and technology issues. 'He was enthusiastic,' I said, scanning some of his emails, 'and talkative. People genuinely liked him. He often attended nerdy conventions, and though he would be reticent to talk about them at first, if you could pry a little bit out of him, the rest would come out like a flood. He was always tinkering with things. The Legos were his idea, weren't they?'

Garvas stepped up beside me. 'How …'

'He believed in your work,' I continued, narrowing my eyes at one of Panos's posts on a Linux forum. 'But he didn't like your corporate structure, did he?'

'Like a lot of us, he felt that investors were an annoying but necessary part of doing what we loved.' Garvas hesitated. 'He didn't sell us out, Leeds, if that's what you're wondering. He *wouldn't* have sold us out.'

'I agree,' I said, turning around in the chair. 'If this man were going to betray his company, he'd just have posted everything on the internet. I find it highly unlikely that he'd sell your files to some other evil corporation rather than just giving them away.'

Garvas relaxed.

'I'll need that list of your rival companies,' I said. 'And coroner's reports, with photos of the body. Specifics on how the corpse vanished. I'll also want details about where Panos lived, his family, and any non-work friends you know about.'

'So … you're agreeing to help us?'

'I'll find the body, Garvas,' I said, standing. 'But first I'm going to go strangle your employer.'

7

I found Yol sitting alone in a cafeteria, surrounded by clean white tables, chairs of green, red, yellow. Each table sported a jar filled with lemons.

Empty, yet decorated with perky colors, the room felt … as if it were holding its breath. Waiting for something. I waved for my aspects to wait outside, then walked in to confront Yol alone. He'd removed his garish sunglasses; without them, he looked almost like an ordinary business-man. Did he wear the glasses to pretend he was a star, or did he wear them to keep people from seeing those keen eyes of his, so certain and so wily?

'You set me up,' I said, taking a seat beside him. 'Ruth-lessly, like a pro.'

Yol said nothing.

'If this story breaks,' I said, 'and everything about I3 goes to hell, I'll be implicated as part-owner in the company.'

I waited for Ivy to chastise me for the curse, bland though it was. But she was outside.

'You could tell the truth,' Yol said. 'Shouldn't be too hard to prove that you only got your shares today.'

'No good. I'm a story, Yol. An eccentric. I don't get the benefit of the doubt with the press. If I'm connected in any way, no protests will keep me out of the tabloids, and you know it. You gave me shares *specifically* so I'd be in the pot with you, you bastard.'

Yol sighed. He looked far older when you could see his eyes. 'Maybe,' he said, 'I just wanted you to feel like I do. I knew *nothing* of the whole cancer fiasco when I bought this place. They dropped the worst of it on me two weeks ago.'

'Yol,' I said, 'you need to talk to the authorities. This is bigger than me or you.'

'I know. And I am. The feds are sending CDC officials tonight. The engineers are going to be quarantined; I probably will be too. I haven't told anyone else yet. But Stephen, the government is wrong; they're looking at this *wrong*. This isn't about a disease, but about information.'

'The corpse,' I said, nodding. 'How could I3 let this happen? Didn't they consider that he was *literally* a walking hard drive?'

'The body was to be cremated,' Yol said. 'Part of an

in-house agreement. It wasn't supposed to be an issue. And even still, the information might not be easy to get. Everyone here is supposed to encrypt the data they store inside their cells. You've heard of a one-time pad?'

'Sure,' I said. 'Random encryption that requires a unique key to decode. Supposed to be unbreakable.'

'Mathematically, it's the *only* unbreakable form of encryption,' Yol said. 'The process isn't very practical for everyday use, but what people were doing here wasn't about practicality, not yet. Company policy insisted on such encryption – before they put data in their bodies, they encrypt it with a unique key. To read that data, then, you'd need that exact key. We don't have the one Panos used, unfortunately.'

'Assuming he actually followed policy and encrypted his data.'

Yol grimaced. 'You noticed?'

'Not the most interested in security, our deceased friend.'

'Well, we have to hope he used a key – because if he did, the people who have his body won't be able to read what he stored. And we might be safe.'

'Unless they find the key.'

Yol pushed a thick folder toward me. 'Exactly. Before we arrived, I had them print this out for you.'

'And it is?'

'Panos's net interactions. Everything he's done over the last few months – every email sent, every forum post. We haven't been able to find anything in it, but I thought you should have it just in case.'

'You're assuming I'm going to help you.'

'You told Garvas –'

'I told him I'd find the corpse. I'm not sure I'll return it to you when I do.'

'That's fine,' Yol said, standing up, taking his sunglasses out of his pocket. 'We have our data, Stephen. We just don't want it falling into the wrong hands. Tell me you disagree.'

'I'm pretty sure that your hands *are* the wrong hands.' I paused. 'Did you kill him, Yol?'

'Panos? No. As far as I can tell, it really *was* an accident.'

I studied him, and he met my eyes before slipping on the ridiculous sunglasses. Trustworthy? I'd always thought so in the past. He tapped the packet of information. 'I'll see that Garvas and his team get you everything else you asked for.'

'If it were only your company,' I said, 'I'd probably just let you burn.'

'I know that. But people are in danger.'

Damn him. He was right. I stood up.

'You have my number,' Yol said. 'I'll likely be on lock-down here, but I should still be able to talk. You, however, need to make a quick exit before the feds arrive.'

'Fine.' I brushed past him, heading toward the door.

'Finding the decryption key isn't enough,' Yol said after me. 'We don't know how many copies of it there are – and that's assuming Panos even followed encryption protocol in the first place. Find that body, Stephen, and *burn it*. That's what I wish I'd done to this whole building weeks ago.'

I opened the door, stepping out and waving to Ivy, Tobias, and J.C. They fell in with me as we walked.

'J.C.,' I said, 'use that phone of yours. Call the other aspects. Send them to the White Room. We've got work to do.'

PART 2

I've got a lot of aspects. Forty-seven, to be exact, with Arnaud being the latest to join us. I don't usually need all of them – in fact, imagining more than four or five at a time is taxing, something I can't do for long. That limitation is yet another thing that makes my psychologists salivate. A psychotic who finds it more tiring to create his fantasy world than live in the real one?

On occasion, a job comes along that requires extra effort, and I need the attention of a large number of aspects. That's why I made the White Room. Blank walls, floor, and ceiling painted the same uniform matte white; smooth, cool surfaces, unbroken save for lights in the ceiling. Soundproofed and calm, here there were no distractions – nothing to focus on but the dozens of imaginary people who flooded in through the double doors.

I don't consciously choose how my aspects look, but something about me seems to appreciate variety. Lua, a Samoan, was a beefy fellow with a vast smile. He wore sturdy cargo pants and a jacket covered in pockets – appropriate for a survivalist. Mi Won, Korean, was our surgeon and field medic. Ngozi – forensic investigation – was a six-foot-four black woman, while Flip was squat, fat, and often tired.

It went on, and on, and on. They'd joined me slowly, one case at a time, as I'd needed to learn some new skill – packing my overcrowded brain with an increasingly diverse array of proficiencies. They acted just like real people would, chatting in a variety of languages. Audrey looked disheveled; she'd obviously been napping. Clive and Owen wore golfing outfits, and Clive carried a driver over his shoulder. I hadn't realized that Owen had finally gotten him to pick up the sport. Kalyani, decked out in a bright red and gold silk sari, rolled her eyes as J.C. called her 'Achmed' again, but I could tell he was growing fond of her. It was tough *not* to be fond of Kalyani.

'Mister Steve!' Kalyani said. 'How was your date? Fun, I hope?'

'It was a step forward,' I said, looking around the room. 'Have you seen Armando?'

'Oh! Mister Steve.' The diminutive Indian woman took

me by the arm. 'Some of us tried to get him to come down. He refused. He says he is on a hunger strike until his throne is returned to him.'

I winced. Armando was getting worse. Nearby, Ivy gave me a pointed look.

'Mister Steve,' Kalyani said, 'you should have my husband Rahul join us.'

'I've explained this before, Kalyani. Your husband is not one of my aspects.'

'But Rahul is *very* helpful,' Kalyani said. 'He's a photographer, and since Armando is so unhelpful lately …'

'I'll consider it,' I said, which seemed to placate her. Kalyani was new, and didn't yet know how all this worked. I couldn't create new aspects at will, and though many of my aspects spoke of their lives – their families, friends, and hobbies – I never actually *saw* any of this. Good thing too. Keeping track of forty-seven hallucinations is tough enough. If I had to imagine their in-laws too, I just might end up going crazy.

Tobias cleared his throat, trying to draw everyone's attention. That proved to be futile before the jabbering hoard of aspects; getting together at once was too novel, and they were enjoying it. So J.C. pulled out his sidearm and shot once into the air.

The room immediately silenced, then was filled with

the sounds of aspects grousing and complaining as they rubbed their ears. Tobias stepped out of the way of a small trail of dust that floated down from above.

I glared at J.C. 'You realize, genius, that now I'm going to have to imagine a *hole* in the ceiling every time we come in here?'

J.C. gave a little shrug, holstering his weapon. He at least had the decency to look embarrassed.

Tobias patted me on the arm. 'I'll patch the hole,' he told me, then turned to the now-silenced crowd. 'A corpse has been stolen. We have been employed to recover it.'

Ivy walked among the aspects, delivering sheets of paper.

'You'll find the details explained here,' Tobias continued. Though they all knew what I did, sometimes going through the motions of delivering information was better for us all. 'It is important you understand that lives are at stake. Perhaps many lives. We need a plan, and quickly. Get to work.'

Ivy finished distributing the sheets, ending next to me. She handed me the last group of papers.

'I already know the details,' I said.

'Your sheet is different,' Ivy said. 'It's everything you know about I3's rival companies.'

I glanced it over, and was surprised at how much

information it contained. I'd spent the ride here pondering the things Yol had told me, and hadn't read his briefings beyond glancing at the names of the three companies he thought most likely to have stolen the corpse. Well, information about each company was apparently tucked in the back of my brain. I flipped through the pages, thoughtful. I hadn't done any research on biotech companies since Ignacio had … left us. I'd assumed that knowledge like this would have gone with him.

'Thanks,' I said to Ivy.

'No problem.'

My aspects spread through the White Room, each starting to work in his or her own way. Kalyani sat on the floor beside a wall and took out a bright red marker. Dylan paced. Lua sidled up to whomever was closest and started a conversation. Most wrote their ideas, using the walls like whiteboards. Some sketched as they wrote, others had a linear progression of ideas, others kept writing things and crossing them out.

I read through Ivy's pages to refresh my memory, then dug into the material Yol had given me. This included the coroner's report, with pictures of the dead man who did indeed look very dead. Liza herself had filled out the report. Might need to visit her, unfortunately.

Once done reading, I strolled through the room looking

over each aspect's work, Tobias at my side. Some aspects focused on whether or not Yol was playing us. Others – like Ivy – extrapolated from what we knew about Panos, trying to decide where they thought he'd be most likely to hide the data key. Still others worked on the problem of the virus.

After one circuit through the room, I leaned back against the wall and picked up the larger stack of papers Yol had given me – the one that contained the record of Panos's web and email interactions over the last few months. It was thick, but this time I didn't worry about paying conscious attention to what I was reading. I just wanted to do a quick speed read to dump it into my brain so the aspects could play with it.

That still took over an hour. By the time I stood up, stretching, much of the white space in the room was filled with theories, ideas, and – in Marinda's case – large floral patterns and an impressively detailed sketch of a dragon. I clasped my hands behind my back and did another circuit of the room, encouraging those who had gotten bored, asking questions about what they'd written, breaking up a few arguments.

In the midst of it I passed Audrey, who was writing her comments in the middle of the air before her, using her finger instead of a pen.

I stopped and raised an eyebrow at her. 'Taking liberties, I see.'

Audrey shrugged. Self-described as 'curvaceous', she had long dark hair and a pretty face. For an expert in handwriting analysis, her penmanship was awful.

'There wasn't space left on the wall,' Audrey said.

'I'm sure,' I said, looking at her hovering text. A second later a pane of glass appeared in the room where she had been writing, making it seem like she'd been writing on glass all along. I felt a headache coming on.

'Oh, that's no fun,' she said, folding her arms.

'It is what must be, Audrey,' I said. 'There are rules.'

'Rules you made up.'

'Rules we all live by,' I said, 'for our own good.' I frowned, reading what she'd written. 'Biochemistry equations? Since when have you been interested in that?'

She shrugged. 'I figured that somebody ought to do a little studying on the topic, and I had the time, since you pointedly refuse to imagine me a pet.'

I rested my fingers on the pane of glass, looking over her cramped notes. She was trying to figure out the method Panos had used to create the virus. There were large gaps in her diagrams, however – breaks that looked as if they'd been ripped free of the writing. What was left went barely beyond basic chemistry.

'It's not going to work, Audrey,' I said. 'This just isn't something we can do anymore.'

'Shouldn't it still be in there, somewhere?'

'No. It's gone.'

'But –'

'Gone,' I said firmly.

'You are one messed-up person.'

'I'm the sanest one in this room.'

'Technically,' she said, 'you're also the most insane.'

I ignored the comment, squatting down beside the pane of glass, inspecting some other notations she'd made on other topics. 'Searching for patterns in the things Panos wrote online?'

'I thought there might be hidden messages in his forum posts,' Audrey explained.

I nodded. When I'd studied handwriting analysis – and, in doing so, created Audrey – I'd done a little tangential research into cryptography. The two disciplines moved in the same circles, and some of the books I'd read had described decoding messages by noticing intentional changes in handwriting, such as a writer crossing some of their *T*s at a different slant to convey hidden information.

That meant Audrey had some small cryptography expertise. More than any of the rest of us did. 'This could be useful,' I said, tapping the pane of glass.

'Might be more useful,' she noted, 'if I – you – had any *real* understanding of cryptography. Do you have time to download some more books, perhaps?'

'You just want to go on more missions,' I said, standing.

'Are you kidding? You get *shot at* on those missions.'

'Only once in a while.'

'Often enough. I'm not so comfortable with being imaginary that I want to see you dead on the ground. You're literally my whole world, Steve-O.' She paused. 'Though, to be honest, I've always been curious what would happen if you took LSD ...'

'I'll see what I can do about the cryptography,' I said. 'Continue with the analysis of his forum posts. Stop with the chemistry sham.'

She sighed, but reached out and started to erase the equations with her sleeve. I walked away, pulling out my phone and bringing up some books on cryptography. If I studied further, would I create another aspect? Or would Audrey really acquire the ability, as she implied? I wanted to say the first was more likely, but Audrey – as the most self-aware of all my aspects – got away with things I wouldn't have expected.

Tobias joined me as I sorted through the volumes available electronically.

'Report?' I asked him.

'General consensus is that this technology is viable,' Tobias said, 'and the threat is real, though Mi Won wants to think more about the effects of dumping rampant DNA strains into the body's muscles. J.C. says we'll want to confirm independently that I3 is in lockdown and that the feds are really involved. That will tell us a great deal about how honest Mister Chay is being with us.'

'Good idea. What's that contact we have at Homeland Security?'

'Elsie,' Tobias said. 'You found her cat.'

Yes, her cat. Not all of my missions involve terrorists or the fate of the world. Some are far more simple and mundane. Like locating a teleporting cat.

'Give her a call,' I said absently. 'See if she'll confirm for us what Yol said about contacting the authorities.'

Tobias stopped beside me. 'Call her?'

I looked up from my screen, then blushed. 'Right. Sorry. I've been talking to Audrey.' She tended to throw me off-balance.

'Ah, dearest Audrey,' Tobias said. 'I sincerely think she must be some kind of compensating factor in your psychology, a way to blow off a little steam, so to speak. Genius is often accompanied by quirks of the mind. Why, Nikola Tesla had an arbitrary, and baffling, aversion to *pearls* of all things. He'd send people away who came to him wearing them, and it is said …'

He continued on. I relaxed to the sound of his voice, choosing a book on advanced cryptography. Tobias eventually wound back around to his report on what the aspects had determined. 'This brings us to our next course of action,' he said. 'Owen's suggestion is perhaps the most relevant, and Ivy won't be able to complete her psychological analysis unless we know more about the subject. Beginning by visiting Panos's family is advised. From there, Ngozi needs more information from the coroner. We may want to go there next.'

'Reverse those,' I said. 'It's … what, three in the morning?'

'Six.'

'Already?' I said, surprised. I didn't feel that tired. The engagement of a new mission, a puzzle to solve, kept me alert. 'Well, still. I feel more comfortable about visiting a coroner's office this early than I do about waking Panos's family. Liza gets to work at … what, seven?'

'Eight.'

So I had time to kill. 'What leads do we have on the corporations who might be behind this?'

'J.C. has some thoughts. He wants to talk to you.'

I found him leaning against the wall near where Ivy was working; he was chattering away and generally distracting her. I grabbed him by the shoulder and pulled him away. 'Tobias said you have something for me.'

'Our assassin,' he said. 'Zen Rigby.'

'Yes, and?' J.C. couldn't have any new information on her – he only knew what I knew, and we'd dredged that well already.

'I've been thinking, Skinny,' J.C. said. 'Why did she show up when you were on your date?'

'Because her employers knew Yol was likely to go to me.'

'Yeah, but why start surveillance on you that early? Look, they have the body, right?'

'So we assume.'

'Therefore, the reason to watch you is to tail you and see if you find the data key. There was no reason to watch you *before* Yol arrived. It tipped their hand, you see? They should have waited until you were called in to I3.'

I chewed on that for a minute. We liked to make fun of J.C., but the truth was, he was one of my most practical aspects. A lot of them spent their days dreaming and thinking. J.C. kept me alive.

'It does seem odd,' I agreed. 'But what does it mean?'

'It means we don't have all the facts,' J.C. said. 'Zen might have been trying to bug us, for instance, hoping we'd go to I3 and reveal information.'

I looked at him sharply. 'Wardrobe change?'

'Good place to start,' he said. 'But there are a host of other reasons she could have been there so early. Perhaps she's employed by a *third* company that knows something is up with I3, but doesn't quite know what. Or maybe she's not involved in this case at all.'

'You don't believe that.'

'I don't,' he agreed. 'But let's tread lightly, eh? Zen is dangerous. I ran across her a couple of times in black ops missions. She left corpses, sometimes operatives – sometimes just innocent bystanders.'

I nodded.

'You'll want to carry a sidearm,' J.C. said. 'You realize that if it comes to a confrontation, I won't be able to shoot her.'

'Because of past familiarity?' I said, giving him an out. I didn't like to push him to confront what he was – instead offering reasons why, despite being my bodyguard, he could never actually interact with anyone we met.

Except that one time when he had done just that.

'Nah,' J.C. said. 'I can't shoot her because I'm not really here.'

I started. Had he just … ? 'J.C.,' I said. 'This is a big step for you.'

'Nah, I've got this figured out. That Arnaud guy, he's pretty smart.'

'Arnaud?' I looked across the room toward the slender, balding Frenchman who was our newest addition.

'Yeah,' J.C. said, hand on my shoulder. 'He has this theory, see. That we're not figments, or whosits, or whatever crazy term you feel like using at the moment. He said ... well, it's a lot of nerd talk, but it means I'm a real boy for sure. I'm just not here.'

'Is that so?' I wasn't certain what to think of this.

'Yup,' J.C. said. 'You should hear what he has to say. Hey, chrome-dome!'

Arnaud pointed at himself, then hustled over as J.C. waved. J.C. put his hand around the diminutive Frenchman, as if they were best friends – the gesture seemed to make Arnaud distinctly uncomfortable. It was a little like the cat buddying up to the mouse.

'Let him have it,' J.C. said.

'It? What it are you speaking of?' Arnaud spoke with a smooth French accent, like butter melting over a browned game hen.

'You know,' J.C said. 'The things you said about us?'

Arnaud adjusted his spectacles. 'Well, um, you see, in quantum physics we talk about possibilities. One interpretation says that dimensions are infinite, and everything that can happen, has happened. It seems to follow if this is true, then each of us aspects somewhere has existed in some dimension or realm of possibility as a real person. A curious thought, would you not agree, Étienne?'

'Curious indeed,' I said. 'It –'

'So I'm real,' J.C. interjected. 'The smart guy just said it.'

'No, no,' Arnaud said. 'I merely indicated that it is likely that somewhere, in another place and time, there really is a person who matches –'

J.C. shoved him aside and wrapped his arm around my shoulders, turning me away from Arnaud. 'I've got it figured out, Skinny. We're all from this other place, see. And when you need some help, you reach out and *snatch* us. You're some kind of physics wizard.'

'A … physics wizard?'

'Yup. And I'm no Navy SEAL. I've just got to accept that.' He paused. 'I'm an Interdimensional Time Ranger.'

I looked at him, grinning.

But he was dead serious.

'J.C.,' I said. 'That's as ridiculous as Owen's ghost theory.'

'No it's not,' J.C. said, stubborn. 'Look, back in that Jerusalem mission. What happened there at the end?'

I hesitated. I had been surrounded, hands shaking, holding a gun I barely knew how to use. In that moment, J.C. had *taken hold* of my arm and directed it, causing me to fire my gun in the precise pattern needed to bring down every enemy.

'I learn quickly,' I said. 'Physics, math, languages … I just need to spend a short time studying, and I can become an expert – via an aspect. Maybe gunplay isn't different. I studied it, fired a few times at the range, and became an expert. But this skill is different – you can't help me by talking – so I couldn't use you properly until I imagined you guiding me. It's not so different from what Kalyani does in guiding me through a conversation in another language.'

'You're stretching,' J.C. said. 'Why hasn't this worked for any other skill you've tried?'

I didn't know.

'I'm a Time Ranger,' J.C. said stubbornly.

'If that were true – which it's *not* – wouldn't you be angry at me for grabbing you from your other life and trapping your quantum ghost here?'

'Nah,' J.C. said. 'It's what I signed up for. The creed of the Time Ranger. We have to protect the universe, and for now that means protecting you as best I can.'

'Oh, for the love of –'

'Hey,' J.C. interrupted. 'Aren't we tight for time? You should be moving.'

'We can't do much until morning arrives,' I said, but allowed myself to be moved on from the topic. I waved Tobias over. 'Keep everyone working. I'm going to go take a shower and do some reading. After that, we're hitting the field.'

'Will do,' Tobias said. 'And the field team is?'

'Standard,' I said. 'You, Ivy, J.C., and …' I looked through the room. 'And we'll see who else.'

Tobias gave me a curious look.

'Have the team meet me in the garage, ready to go, at seven thirty.'

9

I turned the cryptography book to text-to-voice, cranked the volume, and set it to 5x speed. The following shower was long and refreshing. I didn't think about the problem – I just learned.

When I stepped into my bedroom in my bathrobe, I found that Wilson had set out breakfast for me, along with a tall glass of lemonade. I sent him a text, asking him to have the driver prep the SUV – much less conspicuous than taking the limo – for a seven thirty departure.

I finished the book while eating, then made a call to Elsie, my contact in Homeland Security. I woke her up, unfortunately, but she was still willing to check on the matter for me. I put in a call to the coroner's office – got the voicemail, but left a message for Liza – and as I was finishing, got a text back from Elsie. I3 was indeed under lockdown, with the CDC investigating and the FBI involved.

I strode into the garage a short time later, dressed and somewhat refreshed, right on time for our departure. There I found Wilson himself – square-faced, bifocaled, and graying on top – flicking a speck of something off a chauffeur's cap, which he proceeded to put on his head.

'Wait,' I said. 'Isn't Thomas supposed to be in this morning?'

'Unfortunately,' Wilson said, 'he is not coming to work today. Or ever, apparently, as per his message this morning.'

'Oh, no,' I said. 'What happened?'

'You do not recall explaining to him that you were a Satanist, Master Leeds?'

'Two percent Satanist,' I said. 'And Xavier is very progressive for a devil-worshiper. He's never made me sacrifice anything other than imaginary chickens.'

'Yes, well …'

I sighed. Another servant lost. 'We can call in a driver for the day. We had a long night last night. You don't need to do work this early.'

'I don't mind,' Wilson said. 'Somebody needs to look out for you, Master Leeds. Did you sleep at all?'

'Uh …'

'I see. And did you happen to eat anything at dinner last night before you ended up in the tabloids?'

'The story is out already, is it?'

'Written up in the *Mag* and posted on *Squawker* this morning – along with an exposé by Miss Bianca herself. You skipped dinner, and you skipped lunch yesterday as well, insisting that you didn't want to spoil your appetite for the date.'

More like didn't want to throw up from nervousness. 'No wonder that breakfast tasted so good.' I reached for the door handle to the SUV.

Wilson rested his hand on my arm. 'Do not become so preoccupied with saving the world, Master Leeds, that you forget to take care of yourself.' He patted my arm, then climbed into the driver's seat.

My team waited inside, all but Audrey, who burst into the garage wearing a sweater and a scarf. No other aspect had appeared upon my reading the book; Audrey had gained the knowledge, as she'd expected. I was glad – each new aspect put a strain on me, and I'd rather have old ones learn new things. Though, having Audrey along on the mission could be its own special brand of difficult.

'Audrey,' I said as I opened the door for her, 'it's almost June. A scarf?'

'Well,' she said with a grin, 'what good is being imaginary if you can't ignore the weather?' She threw her scarf dramatically over one shoulder, then piled into the car, elbowing J.C. on her way past.

'If I shoot you, woman,' he growled at her, 'it will hurt. My bullets can affect interdimensional matter.'

'Mine can go around corners,' she said. 'And make flowers grow.' She settled in between Ivy and Tobias, and didn't put on her seat belt.

This was going to be an interesting mission.

We pulled out onto the roadway. Morning was upon us, the day bright, and rush hour well under way. I watched out the window, lost in thought for a time, until I noticed J.C. fishing in Ivy's purse.

'Uh …' I said.

'Don't turn,' J.C. said, batting away Ivy's hand as she tried to snatch the purse back. He came out with her compact makeup mirror and held it up to glance over his shoulder out the back window, not wanting to present his profile.

'Yeah,' he said, 'someone's probably following us.'

'Probably?' Ivy asked.

'Hard to say for certain,' J.C. said, shifting the mirror. 'The car doesn't have a front license plate.'

'You think it's her?' I asked. 'The assassin?'

'Again,' J.C. said, 'no way to tell for certain.'

'Maybe there is a way,' Audrey said, tapping her head and the new knowledge inside of it. 'Wanna try some hacking, Steve-O?'

'Hacking?' Ivy said. 'As in computer hacking?'

'No, as in coughing,' Audrey said, rolling her eyes. 'Here, I'm going to write some instructions for you.'

I watched with curiosity as she scribbled down a list of instructions, then handed them to me. It was imaginary paper – not that I could tell. I took it and read the instructions, then glanced at Audrey.

'Trust me,' Audrey said.

'I only read you one book.'

'It was enough.'

I studied her, then shrugged and got out my phone. Worth a try. Following her instructions, I called up F.I.G, the restaurant where I'd eaten – or, well, ordered food – last night. It rang, and fortunately the breakfast staff was already in. An unfamiliar voice answered, asking, 'Hello?'

I followed Audrey's instructions. 'Yeah, hey,' I said. 'My wife ate there last night – but we had a family emergency, and she had to run before finishing her food. In fact, she was in such a hurry, she used the business credit card to pay instead of our home one. I was wondering if I could swap the cards.'

'Okay,' the woman on the phone said. 'What's the name?'

'Carol Westminster,' I said, using the alias Zen had used for her reservation.

A few minutes passed. Hopefully the receipts from last night were still handy. Indeed, after shuffling about a moment, the woman came back on the phone. 'Okay, what's the new card name?'

'Which one did she use?'

'It's a KeyTrust card,' the woman said, starting to sound suspicious. 'Ends in 3409.'

'Oh!' I replied. 'Well, that's the right one after all. Thanks anyway.'

'Great, thanks.' The woman sounded annoyed as she hung up the phone. I wrote the number down in my pocket notebook.

'You call that hacking?' J.C. said. 'What was the point?'

'Wait and see,' Audrey said.

I was already dialing the bank's credit card fraud prevention number. We continued in the car, taking an exit onto the southbound highway as I listened to holding music. Beside me, J.C. kept an eye on our supposed tail with Ivy's mirror. He nodded at me. They'd followed us onto the highway.

When I finally got through the menus, holding patterns, and warnings my call might be recorded, I ended up with a nice-sounding man with a Southern accent on the other side of the line. 'How can I help you?' he asked.

'I need to report a stolen credit card,' I said. 'My wife's

purse got taken from our house last night.'

'All right. Name on the card?'

'Carol Westminster.'

'And the card number?'

'I don't have it,' I said, trying to sound exasperated. 'Did you miss the part about the card being lost?'

'Sir, you just need to look online –'

'I tried! All I can see are the last four digits.'

'You need to –'

'Someone could be spending my money *right now*,' I cut in. 'Do we have time for this?'

'Sir, you have fraud protection.'

'I'm sorry, I'm sorry. I'm just worried. It's not your fault. I just don't know what to do. Please, you can help, right?'

The man on the other line breathed out, as if my tone change indicated he'd just dodged a potentially frustrating incident. 'Just tell me the last four digits, then,' he said, sounding more relaxed.

'The computer says 3409.'

'Okay, let's see … Do you know your PIN number, Mister Westminster?'

'Uh …'

'Social security number attached to the card?'

'805-31-3719,' I said with confidence.

There was a pause. 'That doesn't match our records, sir.'

'But it *is* my social security number.'

'The number I have is probably your wife's, sir.'

'Why does that matter?'

'I can't let you make changes until I authenticate, sir,' the man said in the neutral, patient voice of one accustomed to talking on the phone all day to people who deserved to be strangled.

'Are you *sure?*' I asked.

'Yes, sir. I'm sorry.'

'Well, I suppose you could call her,' I said. 'She's off to work, and I don't have her social handy.'

'I can do that,' the man said. 'Is the number we have on file all right?'

'Which one is that?' I asked. 'Her cell was in her purse.'

'555-626-9013.'

'Drat,' I said, writing down quickly. 'That's the stolen phone's number. I'll just have to call her when she gets to work and have her call you.'

'Very well. Is there anything else, sir?'

'No. Thank you.'

I hung up, then rotated the pad to display the number to the others. 'The assassin's phone number.'

'Great,' J.C. said. 'Now you can ask her out.'

I turned the pad around and looked at the number. 'You know, it was shocking how easy that was, all things considered.'

'Rule number one of decryption,' Audrey said. 'If you don't have to break the code, don't. People are usually far less secure than the encryption strategies they employ.'

'So what do we do with this?' I asked.

'Well, first there's a little app I need you to download onto your phone,' Audrey said. 'J.C., which of the three competitors do you think is most likely to have hired the woman?'

'Exeltec,' J.C. said without missing a heartbeat. 'Of the three, they're the most desperate. Years of funding with no discernible progress, investors breathing down their necks, and a history of moral ambiguity and espionage. Subject of three investigations, but no conclusive findings.'

'That packet has their CEO's phone numbers,' Audrey said.

I smiled and started working on the phone. In short time, I had my mobile set up to send fake information to Zen's caller ID, indicating I was Nathan Haight, owner of Exeltec.

'Have Wilson ready to honk,' Audrey said.

I told him to be ready, then dialed.

It rang once. Twice.

Then picked up.

'Here,' a curt, female voice said. 'What is it? I'm busy.'

I gestured to Wilson. He honked loudly.

I heard it over the phone as well. Zen was most certainly tailing us. I hit the button on my phone's app that imitated static on the line, then said something, which I knew would be distorted beyond recognition.

Zen cursed, then she said, 'I don't care how nervous the other partners are. Bothering me repeatedly isn't going to make this go faster. I'll call in with a report when I know something. Until then, leave me alone.'

She hung up.

'That,' J.C. said, 'was the strangest hacking I've ever seen.'

'That's because you don't know what hacking really is,' Audrey said, sounding smug. 'You imagine geeks in front of a computer. But in reality, most people "hacking" today – at least as far as the media calls it – just spend their time on the phone trying to pry out information.'

'So we know she's following us,' Ivy said, '*and* we know the name of our rival company. Which tells us who has the corpse.'

'Not for certain,' I said. 'But it looks good.' I tapped my phone, thoughtful, as Wilson pulled off the highway and started driving through downtown. 'Advice?'

'We need to avoid getting in over our heads,' Ivy said. 'If that's humanly possible for us.'

'I agree,' Tobias said. 'Stephen, if we can find proof that Exeltec stole the body, the CDC might be willing to raid their offices.'

'We could just raid their offices ourselves,' J.C. said. 'Cut out the middleman.'

'I'd rather not do anything specifically illegal,' Tobias replied.

'Don't worry,' J.C. said. 'As an Interdimensional Time Ranger, I have code 876 special authorization to ignore local legal statutes in times of emergency. Look, Skinny, we're going to end up compromising Exeltec eventually. I can feel it. Even if they aren't storing the body in their local offices, there will be a trail to it in there somewhere.'

'For what it's worth,' Audrey added. 'I'm with J.C. Breaking in sounds like fun.'

I sat back, thinking. 'We'll go to the coroner,' I finally said, getting a nod from Tobias and Ivy. 'I'd rather find proof incriminating Exeltec, and then set up an official raid.' A plan was beginning to form in my head. 'Besides,' I added, 'breaking in isn't the *only* way to find out what Exeltec knows …'

10

The car rolled down a waking urban street, lamps flickering off now that the sun was fully up, like servants lowering their heads before their king. The city morgue was near the hospital, situated in a spread-out office complex that could have easily held three or four exciting internet start-ups. We passed carefully-trimmed hedges and trees with last year's Christmas lights still wrapped around them, dormant until the season started up again.

'All right,' J.C. said to me. 'You ready for this?'

'Ready?' I said.

'We're being tailed by an assassin, Skinny,' he said. 'That feeling between your shoulder blades, that's the knowledge that someone has you in their sights. She could squeeze the trigger at any moment.'

'Don't be silly,' Ivy said. 'She's not going to hurt us

as long as she thinks we're leading her to important information.'

'Are you sure?' J.C. said. 'Because I'm not. At any moment, her higher-ups could decide that you working for Yol is a very, very bad thing. They could decide to remove the competition and take their chances at finding the key on their own.'

The way he said it, cold and straightforward, made me squirm.

'You just don't like being followed,' Ivy said.

'Damn right.'

'Language.'

'Look,' J.C. said, 'Zen has information we'd really like to know. If we capture her, that alone might give us the proof we need. We know where she is, and we have a momentary advantage. How well do you think you could pull off a quiet evacuation?'

'Not well,' I said.

'Let's try it anyway,' J.C. said, pointing. 'See that turn right ahead, as we move into the parking lot? The hedge there will hide us from the view of the car following us. You need to bail from the vehicle there – don't worry, I'll help you – and have Jeeves park in front of the building right beside the hedges. We can get the drop on Zen and turn this chase on its head.'

'Reckless,' Ivy said.

It was, but as the turn approached, I made a decision. 'Let's do it,' I said. 'Wilson, I'm slipping out of the car at the next turn. Drive as if nothing has happened; don't slow more than normal. Park right in front of the morgue, then wait.'

He adjusted the rearview mirror so he could meet my eyes. He didn't say anything, but I could see that he was concerned.

The turning of the mirror gave me a good glimpse of the dark sedan behind us. I felt under my jacket for the sidearm J.C. had insisted I bring. This was *not* how I liked missions to go. I'd rather spend ten hours in a room trying to figure out a puzzle or a safe with no lock. Why, lately, did guns always seem to get involved?

I moved to the side door, then crouched down, grabbing the handle. J.C. moved over behind me, hand on my shoulder.

'Five, four, three …' he counted.

I took a deep breath.

'Two … *One!*'

I cracked the door right as Wilson turned the car around the hedge. J.C. *heaved* against my back, somehow pushing me in just the right way so that when I left the car, I hit in a curling roll. It still hurt. The momentum of the car's turn clicked the door shut and I rolled up into a crouch beside the hedge, where I waited until I heard the car behind us start to turn.

I slipped through the hedge to the other side right as the car turned around it, following Wilson. This meant that I was separated from Zen by the squat wall of densely packed foliage. It ran all the way along the parking lot here.

I scurried along the hedge, head down, keeping pace with Zen's car. It passed Wilson as he parked, then continued on in a presumably nonsuspicious way toward another section of the parking lot. I caught brief glimpses of black car through holes in the hedge – a shadowed driver, but nobody else visible. The car pulled into a parking stall a short distance from where the hedge ended.

Ahead, the leaves rustled, and J.C. slipped through, handgun out, joining me. 'Nice work,' he whispered. 'We'll make a Ranger out of you yet.'

'It was your push,' I said. 'Sent me tumbling exactly the right way.'

'I said I'd help.'

I said nothing, too nervous to continue the conversation. I was manifesting something new, an extension of my previous … framework. What else could I learn to do by having one of my aspects guide my fingers or steps?

I peeked through the hedge, then took out my handgun.

J.C. motioned furiously for me to hide it in front of myself, so cars passing along the street to my right wouldn't see. Then J.C. nodded toward an opening in the hedge.

I took a deep breath before scrambling through and crossing the short distance to Zen's car. J.C. tailed me. I came up beside the car in a crouch.

'Ready?' J.C. asked.

I nodded.

'Finger on the trigger, Skinny. This is for real.'

I nodded again. The passenger's side window, just above me, was open. Palms sweating, I threw myself to my feet and leveled my gun through the open window at the driver.

It wasn't the assassin.

11

The driver was a dark-haired kid, maybe eighteen, wearing a hoodie. He cried out, dropping the pair of binoculars he'd been using to look toward my SUV, his face going white as snow as he stared down my handgun.

That was most certainly *not* Zen Rigby.

'In the car, Skinny,' J.C. said, looking around the parking lot. 'Back seat, so he can't grapple you. Tell him to keep quiet. Don't look suspicious.'

'Hands where I can see them,' I told the kid, hoping he didn't see that my gun was shaking. 'Don't say a word.' I pulled open the back door, slipped in, but kept the gun on him.

The kid remained quiet save for a whine in the back of his throat. He was either terrified, or was a very good actor.

'Where's Zen?' I said to him, lifting the gun up beside the youth's head.

'Who?' he said.

'No games. *Where is she?*'

'I don't … I don't know anything …' The kid actually started weeping.

'Damn it,' J.C. said, standing by the front window. 'You think he's acting?'

'No idea,' I said back.

'I should fetch Ivy.'

'No,' I said, not wanting to be left alone. I inspected the kid's weeping face reflected in the rearview mirror. Mediterranean skin tone … Same nose …

'Don't kill me,' the kid whispered. 'I just wanted to know what you did with him.'

'You're Panos's brother,' I guessed.

The kid nodded, still sobbing.

'Oh hell,' J.C. said. 'No wonder it was so easy to spot the tail. *Two* people were following us: an amateur and a professional. I'm an idiot.'

I felt cold. I'd heard Wilson's honk through the line when on the phone with Zen, so she had been nearby, yet we hadn't spotted her. Zen had been invisible to us all along.

Bad.

'What's your name?' I asked the youth.

'Dion.'

'Well, Dion, I'm putting the gun away. If you are who you say, then you don't need to be afraid. I'm going to need you to come with me, and if you start to run, or cry out, or anything like that … well, I'll have to make sure you stop.'

The youth nodded.

I climbed from the car, gun holstered, and pulled the kid out by his shoulder. A quick frisk determined he wasn't armed, though he considered himself quite the spy. Flashlight, ski mask, binoculars, a mobile phone which I took and turned off. I marched him across the parking lot, fully aware that this whole exchange would have looked *very* suspicious to anyone watching. With J.C.'s coaching, though, I maintained the air of someone who knew what he was doing – arm on the youth's shoulder, walking confidently. We were in the government complex; hopefully, anyone who spotted us would think I was a cop.

If they didn't, well, it wouldn't be the first time the police had been called to deal with me. I think they kept a department pool going on the frequency of it.

I shoved Dion into my SUV, then climbed inside, feeling a little more secure with the tinted windows and more of my aspects in attendance. Dion moved to the back seat and slumped there, forcing Audrey to climb onto Tobias's lap – an event so unexpected, the aging aspect almost seemed to choke.

'Wilson, please give me warning if anyone approaches,' I said. 'All right, Dion. Spill it. Why are you following me?'

'They stole Panos's body,' Dion said.

'And by "they" you mean ...'

'I3.'

'And why on earth would they do such a thing?'

'The information,' Dion said. 'He had it stored in his cells, you know? All of their secrets. All the terrible things they were going to do.'

I shared a look with J.C., who then facepalmed. Panos had been talking to his family about his research. Wonderful. J.C. removed his hand and mouthed to me, *security nightmare.*

'And what kind of terrible things,' I said, 'do you assume I3 was going to do?'

'I ...' Dion looked to the side. 'You know. *Corporate* things.'

'Like take away casual Fridays,' Audrey guessed.

So Panos hadn't completely confided in his brother. I tapped my fingers on the armrest. The family assumed that Yol and his people had taken the body to keep their information hidden – and, to be honest, that wasn't far from the truth. They'd been planning to see it burned, after all. Someone had merely gotten to Panos first.

'And you're following me,' I said to the kid. 'Why?'

'You were all over the internet this morning,' Dion said. 'Getting into a car with that weird Asian guy who owns I3. I figured out that you were supposed to crack the code on Panos's body. Seems obvious. I mean, you're some kind of superspy hacker or something, right?'

'That's *exactly* what we are,' Audrey said. 'Steve-O, tell him that's what we are.' When I said nothing, she elbowed Tobias, in whose lap she was still sitting. 'Tell him, grandpa.'

'Stephen,' Tobias said, somewhat uncomfortable, 'this youth sounds earnest.'

'He's being honest,' Ivy said, inspecting him, 'so far as I can tell.'

'You should reassure him,' Tobias said. 'Look at the poor lad. He looks like he still thinks you're going to shoot him.'

Indeed, Dion had his hands clasped, eyes down, but he was trembling.

I softened my tone. 'I wasn't hired to crack the body's code,' I told him. 'I3 has plenty of backups on all their information. I'm here to find the corpse.'

Dion looked up.

'No,' I said, 'I3 didn't take it. They would have been perfectly content to let it be cremated.'

'I don't think he believes you, Steve,' Ivy said.

'Look,' I said to Dion, 'I don't care what happens with I3. I just want to make sure the information in that corpse is accounted for, all right? And for now, I need you to wait here.'

'Why –'

'Because I don't know what to do with you.' I glanced at Wilson, who nodded. He'd keep an eye on the kid. 'Go climb in the front seat,' I told Dion. 'When I get back, we can have a long conversation about all of this. For now, I have to go deal with a very surly coroner.'

12

The city coroner was housed in a sterile-smelling little office beside the city morgue, which was only one set of rooms in a larger medical complex. Technically, Liza liked to be called a 'medical examiner,' and she was always surprisingly busy for a person who seemed to spend all of her time playing internet games.

At the stroke of eight, I strode through the medical complex lobby – suffering the glare of a security guard who was far too large for the little cubby they'd given him – and knocked politely on the coroner's office door. Liza's secretary – I forget his name – opened the door with an obviously reluctant expression.

'She's waiting for you,' the young man said. 'I wouldn't call her excited, though.'

'Great. Thanks …'

'John,' Tobias filled in.

'… John.'

The secretary nodded, walking back to his desk and shuffling papers. I strolled down a short hallway to a nice office, hung with official-looking diplomas and the like. I managed to get a glimpse of Facebook reflected in one of them as Liza turned off her tablet and looked up at me.

'I'm busy, Leeds,' she said.

Dressed in a white labcoat over jeans and a pink buttoned blouse, Liza was in her late fifties, and was tall enough that she was very tired of answering whether or not she'd played basketball in school. It was fortunate her clients were, for the most part, dead – as that was the only type of person who didn't seem to bother her.

'Well, this shouldn't take long,' I said, leaning against the doorframe and folding my arms, partially to block Tobias's adoring stare. What he saw in the woman, I'd never know.

'I don't have to do anything for you,' Liza said, making a good show of turning toward her computer screen, as if she had tons and tons of work to do. 'You're not involved in any kind of official case. Last I heard, the department had decided not to involve you anymore.'

She said that last part a touch too triumphantly. Ivy and J.C. shared a look. The authorities weren't … particularly fond of us these days.

'One of your bodies went missing,' I said to her. 'Isn't anyone worried about that?'

'Not my problem,' Liza said. 'My part was done. Death pronounced, identity confirmed, no autopsy required. The morgue had a lapse. Well, you can talk to them about it.'

Not a chance. They wouldn't let me in – they didn't have the authority. But Liza could; this *was* her department, no matter what she said.

'And the police aren't concerned about the breach?' I asked. 'Sergeant Graves hasn't been poking around, wondering how such a terrible security snafu happened?'

Liza hesitated.

'Ah,' Ivy said. 'Good guess, Steve. Push more there.'

'This is your division,' I said to Liza. 'Don't you even want to know how it happened? I can help.'

'Every time you "help", Leeds, some kind of catastrophe follows.'

'Seems like a catastrophe already happened.'

'Hit her where it hurts,' Ivy said. 'Mention the hassle.'

'Think of the paperwork, Liza,' I said. 'A body missing. Investigations, questions, people poking around, *meetings you'll have to attend*.'

Liza couldn't completely cover her sour grimace. Beside me, Ivy grinned in satisfaction.

'All this,' Liza said, leaning back, 'for a body that should never have been here.'

'What do you mean?' I asked.

'There was no *reason* for us to keep the corpse. Kin had identified him; no foul play was suspected. I should have released the body to the family's chosen mortician for embalming. But no. Not allowed. This corpse had to stay here, and nobody would tell me why. The commissioner himself insisted.' She narrowed her eyes at me. 'Now you. What was special about that guy, Leeds?'

The commissioner? Yol had done some work to keep this body in custody. Made sense. If he'd had the corpse released, then given it some kind of crazy security, that would have advertised to the world that there was something special about it. A quick call to ensure Panos stayed in the city morgue, locked up tight, was far less suspicious.

It just hadn't worked.

'We're going to have to give something up, Steve,' Ivy told me. 'She's digging her heels in. Time for the big guns.'

I sighed. 'You sure?' I asked under my breath.

'Yes, unfortunately.'

'One interview,' I said, meeting Liza's eyes. 'One hour.'

She leaned forward in her chair. 'Buying me off?'

'Yes, and?'

She tapped the top of her table with an idle finger. 'I'm a medical examiner. I'm not interested in publishing.'

'I didn't say the interview had to be with you,' I said. 'Anyone you like – anyone in the medical community you need something from. *You* get *me* as barter.'

Liza smiled. 'Anyone?'

'Yes. One hour.'

'No. As long as they want.'

'That's too open-ended, Liza.'

'So is the list of ways you're annoying. Take it or leave it, Leeds. I don't owe you anything.'

'We're going to regret this, aren't we?' Tobias asked.

I nodded, thinking of the hours spent being prodded by some psychologist who was looking to make a name for themselves. Another paper in another journal, treating me like a strange species of sea cucumber to be dissected and displayed.

Time was ticking though, and it was either this or tell Liza why the body was so important.

'Deal,' I said.

She didn't smile. Smiling was far too human an expression for Liza. She did seem satisfied, though, as she grabbed her keys off the table and led me down the hallway, my aspects trailing.

The air grew appreciably colder as we approached the

morgue. A key card unlocked the door, which was of heavy, thick metal. Inside the room, one could see why Liza had chosen to work here – not only was it frigid, all this chrome probably reminded her of the spaceship that had dropped her off on our planet.

The door swung closed behind us, thumping into place. Liza settled in beside the wall, arms folded, watching to prevent any shenanigans. 'Fifteen minutes, Leeds. Get to it.'

I surveyed the room, which had three metal tables on wheels, a counter with various medical paraphernalia, and a wall full of large corpse drawers.

'All right,' I said to the four aspects, 'I want to know how they got the body out.'

'We need proof too,' J.C. said, poking through the room. 'Something to tie Exeltec to the crime.'

'That would be wonderful,' I said to him, 'but honestly, we don't want to be too leading. Maybe they don't have it. Focus on what we know. Find me clues on how the thieves stored or moved the body, and that might lead us right to it.'

The others nodded. I turned around slowly, taking the whole room in, absorbing it into my subconscious. Then I closed my eyes.

My delusions started talking.

'No windows,' J.C. said. 'Only one exit.'

'Unless those ceiling tiles are removable,' Ivy noted.

'Nah,' J.C. replied. 'I've seen the security specs for this building. Remember the Coppervein case? No crawl space. No air ducts. Nothing funny about the architecture.'

'This equipment *has* been used lately,' Tobias said. 'I know little of its purpose, though. Stephen, you really *should* recruit a coroner of our own eventually.'

'We *do* have Ngozi,' Audrey said. 'Forensic investigation. Why didn't we bring her?'

Because of you, Audrey, I thought. *My subconscious gave you an important skill and inserted you into my team.* Why? I missed the days when I'd had someone to ask about things like this. When Sandra had been with me, everything had made sense for the first time in my life.

'This place is secure,' Ivy said, sounding dissatisfied. 'Inside job, perhaps? One of the morgue workers?'

'Could one of the workers here have been bribed?' I asked, opening my eyes and looking toward Liza.

'I thought of that,' she said, arms still folded. 'But I was the last one in the office that night. I came in, checked everything and turned off the lights. Security says nobody came in overnight.'

'I'll want to talk to security, then,' I said. 'Who else was here that day?'

Liza shrugged. 'Family. A priest. Always accompanied.

This room doesn't open for anyone other than me and two of our technicians. Even the security guard can't get in without calling one of us. But that's all irrelevant – the body was still here when I left for the night.'

'You're sure?'

'Yeah, I had to write down some numbers for paperwork. I checked on it specifically.'

'We'll want to fingerprint the place,' J.C. said. 'Like it or not, we might have to go through the precinct.'

I nodded. 'I assume the police have already done forensics.'

'Why would you assume that?' Liza asked.

We all looked at her. 'Uh … you know. Because there was a *crime*?'

'A corpse was stolen,' Liza said dryly. 'Nobody was hurt, we have no actual signs of a break-in, and there is no money involved. The official word is that they are "work-ing" on the case, but let me tell you – finding this body is low on their list of priorities. They're more worried about the break-in itself; they'll want someone's hide for that …'

She refolded her arms, then repositioned and folded them again. She was trying to play it cool, but she *was* obviously worried. Ivy nodded at me, obviously pleased that I could read Liza so well. Well, it wasn't hard. I picked up things from my aspects now and then.

'Security cameras?' J.C. asked as he inspected the corners of the room. I repeated the question so Liza could hear it.

'Just out in the hallways,' she said.

'Isn't that a little sparse?' I asked.

'The whole place is wired with alarms. If someone tries to break in, the security guard's desk will light up like Christmas.' She grimaced. 'We used to turn it on only at night, but they've had it on for two days straight now. Have to get permission to open a damn window these days …'

I looked at the team.

'Stephen,' Tobias said, 'we're going to need Ngozi.'

I sighed. Well, it wasn't *too* long a drive to go back and pick her up.

'Here,' J.C. said, pulling out his phone. 'Let me give her a call.'

'I don't think …' I said, but he was already dialing.

'Yeah, Achmed, we need your help,' he said. 'What? Of course I have your number. No, I have *not* been stalking you. Look, can you find Ngozi? How should I know where she is? Probably washing her hands a hundred times or something. No, I have *not* been stalking her either.' He lowered the phone, giving the rest of us a suffering look. He raised it back up, and a short time later, continued. 'Great. Let's video conference.'

Tobias and I looked over J.C.'s shoulders as Kalyani's face appeared on the screen, perky and excited. She waved, then turned the phone toward Ngozi, who sat reading on her bed.

What to say about Ngozi? She was from Nigeria, with deep brown skin, and had been educated at Oxford. She was also deathly afraid of germs – so much so that when Kalyani held the phone toward her, Ngozi shied away visibly. She shook her head, and Kalyani was obliged to stand there, holding the phone.

'What's up?' Ngozi asked with a clipped Nigerian accent.

'Crime scene investigation,' I said.

'You're going to come get me?'

'Well, I guess we kind of thought …' I hesitated, then looked to J.C. 'I don't know if this is going to work, J.C. We've never done anything like this before.'

'Worth a try, though, right?'

I looked toward Ivy, who seemed skeptical, but Tobias shrugged. 'What harm can it do, Stephen? Getting Ngozi out of the house is difficult sometimes.'

'I heard that,' Ngozi said. 'It's not *difficult*. I just require proper preparation.'

'Yeah,' J.C. said, 'like a hazmat suit.'

'Please,' Ngozi said, rolling her eyes. 'Just because I like things clean.'

'Clean?' I asked her.

'Very clean. Do you know the kinds of poisons that are pumped into the air every day by all those cars and factories? Where do you think that all goes? Do you ever wonder what that crusty blackness is on your skin after you hold a handrail on your way down the steps into the subway? And think of the *people*. Coughing into their hands, wiping their snotty nostrils, touching everything and everyone, and –'

'We get it, Ngozi,' I said. I looked at Tobias, who nodded encouragingly. J.C. was right; phones among my aspects could be a valuable resource. I took the phone from J.C. Nearby, Liza watched me with what seemed like the first genuine emotion she'd displayed all morning: Fascination. She might not be a psychologist, but physicians of all varieties tend to find my … quirks captivating.

Good for her. As long as it kept her from thinking about how much – or little – time I had remaining of her original 'fifteen minute' restriction.

'We're going to try this over the phone,' I said to Ngozi. 'We're at the icebox. By all accounts, the body was here at night, but gone the next morning. Nothing suspicious on the hallway security cameras.' Liza nodded when I checked with her on this one. 'There isn't a camera in this room specifically, but the building does have an intense security system. So how did they get the body out?'

Ngozi leaned forward, still not taking the camera from Kalyani, but inspecting me with curiosity. 'Show me the room.'

I walked around it, scanning the place, fully aware that to Liza's perspective, I was holding nothing. Ngozi hummed to herself as I walked. Some show tune; I wasn't certain which one.

'So,' she said after I'd spent a few minutes scanning the place, 'you're sure the body is gone?'

'Of course it's gone,' I said, pointing the camera toward the still-open corpse drawer.

'Well,' Ngozi said, 'it's going to be hard to do any traditional forensics here. But the question we should ask first is, "Do we need to?" You'd be surprised at how often something is reported stolen, only to be found lost – or stashed – someplace very close to where the theft happened. If getting the body out of the room would be so hard, maybe it never did leave the room.'

I looked at the other drawers. Then, with a sigh, I put the phone aside and began pulling them open one at a time. After a few minutes, Liza walked over and helped me. 'We did this,' she mentioned, but didn't stop me from double-checking. Only three of the other drawers had corpses, and we checked each one carefully. None were Panos.

From there, I looked in the room's cabinets, closets, and even drawers that were too small for a corpse. It was a long process, and one that I was actually pleased to find unfruitful. Discovering several bags full of elbows or whatnot wouldn't have been particularly appealing.

I dusted off my hands and looked toward the phone and Ngozi's image. Kalyani had joined her on the bed, and the two had been chatting about how I really *did* need to stop working so much and settle down with someone nice. And, preferably, someone sane.

'What next?' I said to the phone.

'Locard's principle,' Ngozi said.

'Which is?'

'Basically,' she said, 'the principle states that whenever there is contact, or an exchange, evidence is left behind. We have very little to go on, as the victim was already dead when abducted, and presumably still zipped up tight. But the perpetrator will have left behind signs they were here. I don't suppose we can get a DNA sweep of the room …'

I looked hopefully at Liza and asked, to which I got a sniff of amusement. The case wasn't nearly important enough for that. 'We can try for fingerprints on our own,' I said to Ngozi. 'But the police aren't going to help.'

'Let's do obvious contact points first,' Ngozi said. 'Close up on the drawer handle please.'

I brought the phone over and put it very close to the handle of the corpse drawer. 'Great,' Ngozi said after a minute. 'Now the door into the room.'

I did so, passing Liza, who was checking her watch.

'Time might be running out, Ngozi,' I said softly.

'My art isn't exactly something that can be rushed,' she noted back at me. 'Particularly long-distance.'

I showed her the door handle, not really certain what she was looking for. Ngozi had me pull the door open to look at the other side. The door *was* heavy, made to swing shut after anyone who left. Once I was outside, I couldn't open it again. Liza had to unlock it with a key card.

'All right, Leeds,' Liza said as I turned the camera to show the strike plate on the inside of the door frame. 'You –'

'Bingo,' Ngozi said.

I froze in place, then looked back at the door frame. Ignoring the rest of what Liza said, I knelt down, trying to see what Ngozi had.

'See those dust marks?' Ngozi asked.

'Um … no?'

'Look closely. Someone put tape here, then pulled it off, leaving behind enough gum to attract dust.'

Liza stooped down beside me. 'Did you hear me?'

'Tape,' I asked. 'Do you have some tape?'

'Why –'

'Yo,' J.C. said from inside the room, holding up a roll of the translucent industrial tape that lay on the counter.

I brushed past Liza and fetched the tape – J.C. had to set down his imaginary copy before I could see the real one – then rushed back. I placed a strip of it over the strike plate, stepped out of the room, and let the door slide closed.

It thumped into place. That thump covered the lack of a click. When I pushed on the door, it opened without needing help from the inside.

'We know how they got into the room,' I said.

'So?' Liza asked. 'We knew they'd gotten in somehow. How does this help?'

'It tells us it was likely someone who visited the day before the body went missing,' I said. 'The last visitor, perhaps? They would be in a position to tape the door with the least chance of discovery during the day.'

'I'm pretty sure I'd have noticed if the door were taped,' Liza said.

'Would you have? With the key card unlocking, you never have to turn or twist anything. It's natural for you to push the door and have it just swing open.'

She thought about it for a moment. 'Plausible,' she admitted. 'But who did it?'

'Who was last into this room that day?'

'The priest. I had to let him in. The others had gone home for the evening, but I stayed late.'

'Had a FreeCell game that you just *had* to finish?' I asked.

'Shut up.'

I smiled. 'Did you recognize the priest?'

She shook her head. 'But he was on the list and his ID was valid.'

'Creating a fake ID wouldn't be much,' Ivy said to me, 'considering what was at stake.'

'That's probably our man,' I said to Liza. 'Come on, I want to talk to your security officer.'

As Liza pulled the tape off the door, I thanked Ngozi for her help, turned off the camera, and tossed the phone back to J.C.

'Nice work,' Ivy noted to him, smiling.

'Thanks,' he said, slipping the phone into a pocket of his cargo pants. 'Of course, it's not *actually* a phone. It's a hyper-dimensional time –'

'J.C.,' Ivy interrupted.

'Yeah?'

'Don't ruin this moment.'

'Oh. Yeah, okay.'

13

I hit the restroom in the hallway before going to the security station. I didn't really need to go to the bathroom, but Tobias did.

The room was clean, which I appreciated. The soap dispensers were full, the mirror spotless, and it even had a little chart on the door listing the last cleaning, where the staff had to sign to prove they'd done their job. I washed my hands, looking at myself in the mirror while Tobias finished his pit stop.

My own mundane face looked back at me. I'm never what people expect. Some picture me as some sort of eccentric scientist, others imagine an action star. Instead, they get a rather bland man in his thirties, perfectly normal.

In some ways, I often feel like my White Room. A blank slate. The aspects have all the character. I try very hard to not stand out. Because I am *not crazy*.

I dried my hands and waited for Tobias to wash up, then we rejoined the others outside and walked toward the security station. It consisted of a circular desk with an open center, the type you'd find at a mall beneath a sign proclaiming 'Information.' I walked up and the security guard looked me over – like I was a piece of pizza and he was trying to decide how long I'd been sitting in the fridge. He didn't ask what I wanted. Liza had called him to tell him to prepare camera footage for me.

The desk really was too small for this hulk of a man. When he leaned forward, the inside front of the desk pressed into his gut; I was left with the impression of a grape being squeezed from the bottom.

'You,' the guard said with a deep baritone voice, 'are the crazy one, aren't you?'

'Well, that's not actually true,' I said. 'You see, the standard definition of insanity is –'

He leaned forward farther, and I pitied the poor desk. 'You're armed.'

'Uh …'

'So am I,' the guard said softly. 'Don't try anything.'

'Okaaay,' Ivy said from beside me. 'Creepy guy manning the security station.'

'I like him,' J.C. said.

'Of course you do.'

The guard slowly lifted a flash drive. 'Footage is on here.'

I took it. 'You're certain the security system was on that night?'

The man nodded. His hand made a fist, as if me even *asking* something so stupid was an offense worthy of a pounding.

'Uh,' I said, watching that fist, 'Liza says you leave it on during the day now, too?'

'I'm going to catch him,' the guard said. 'Nobody breaks into *my* building.'

'Twice,' I said.

The guard eyed me.

'Nobody breaks into your building twice,' I said. 'Since they did it once already. Actually … they might have done it twice already, since the first time they placed the tape on the door – but you might call that more of an infiltration than a break-in.'

'Don't give me lip,' the man said, pointing at me, 'and don't make trouble. Otherwise I'll thump you so hard, it'll knock some of your personalities into the next state.'

'Ouch,' Audrey said, flipping through a magazine she'd found on his desk. 'Ask him why, if he's so amazingly observant, he hasn't noticed that his fly is down.'

I smiled, then made a quick exit. Liza watched me go from the doorway of her office.

Outside, I held up the flash drive, then began moving

along the side of the building. I waved to Wilson, who was still in the car. Panos's brother sat sullenly in the front passenger seat, drinking a glass of lemonade.

I rounded the building, aspects trailing, so we could get a good look at the exterior. It had small windows, maybe large enough to fit through. No fire escape. I approached a back door; it was locked tight. I gave it a good shake anyway.

'Someone impersonated a priest,' I said to the aspects, 'and slipped in to inspect the body and place the tape. Then they came back at night to extract the corpse. So why didn't they just take a sample of the body's cells when they were first there, in the room with it?'

I looked toward the others, who all seemed baffled.

'I guess they didn't know where on the body the modified cells were to be found,' Tobias finally said. 'There are many, many cells in the body. How were they to know which place held the information they wanted?'

'Perhaps.' I folded my arms, dissatisfied. *We're missing something*, I thought. *A very important piece of all this. It* –

The back door burst open. The security guard stood there, puffing, hand on his sidearm. He glared at me.

'I just wanted to check,' I said, inspecting the now-open doorway. Tape wouldn't work here; the door had a deadbolt. 'Nice response time, by the way.'

He poked a finger at me. 'Don't push me.'

He slammed the door. I continued on my way, rounding the corner into a little alleyway between this building and the next, looking for other entrances. I was about halfway down it when I heard the soft click behind me.

I spun, as did my aspects. There stood Zen Rigby beside a large trash bin, holding a paper bag with one hand inside of it, her posture innocent.

'SIG Sauer P239,' J.C. said softly, looking at the bag, which undoubtedly held a gun.

'You can tell the type of gun by the way it sounds to *cock*?' Ivy asked.

'Well yeah,' J.C. said. 'Duh.' He looked embarrassed as he said it, though, and gave me a glance. He felt he should have spotted Zen sneaking up on us. But he could only hear or see what I did.

'Mister Leeds,' the woman said. Like last night, she wore a pantsuit and white blouse. She was dark and short with straight black hair. No jewelry.

I inclined my head toward her.

'I will need you to divest yourself of your sidearm,' Zen said. 'With attention and care, please, lest an unfortunate incident result.'

I glanced at J.C.

'Do it,' he said, though he sounded reluctant. 'She probably won't try to kill us here.'

'Probably?' Audrey asked, looking pale.

I slowly slid my gun out, then leaned down and set it on the ground before kicking it away. Zen smiled, sack still carried in a way that would make it easy to raise and shoot me.

'You called me earlier,' she said. 'A ploy which I must commend. I assume the purpose was to determine if I was following you or not?'

I nodded, hands at my sides, breathing quickly. I found myself in situations like this far too often. I wasn't a soldier or a cop; I wasn't cool under fire. I did *not* like having a gun pointed at me.

'Control the situation, Skinny,' J.C. said from beside me. 'The people who end up dead are the ones who lose control. Don't let your nerves determine how this plays out.'

'Now,' Zen said, 'I'll need that flash drive.'

I blinked. The flash drive …

She thought the flash drive contained the code to unlock Panos's data. How must it look to her? I got hired by Yol, then spent the night working. I headed to the coroner as soon as possible in the morning, then walked out with a flash drive.

She'd guessed that I'd recovered something important. Ivy laughed, though J.C. looked concerned. I glanced at him.

'If she thinks she has what she needs,' he said softly, 'we are in serious danger. If you give her the flash drive, don't go anywhere with her.'

I backed away from Zen, hands still to the sides, until I was against the wall to the building. She studied me. Her gun was probably suppressed, but it would still make a sound. Relatively exposed as we were, she had to be worried about firing.

My heart beat frantically. Control the situation. Get her talking, perhaps? 'Who did you get to impersonate the priest for you?'

She frowned. Then she raised her bag and the gun inside. 'I asked you politely for something, Mister Leeds.'

'And I'm not going to give it to you,' I said. 'Until I at least know how you pulled off the heist. It's a quirk of mine. I'm certain you're aware that I'm prone to those.'

She hesitated. Then she glanced to the sides.

Looking for my aspects, I thought. People did that, unconsciously, when they were around me.

'Good,' Ivy said. 'Playing the insanity card does tend to throw people off their game.'

Think, think, think. I knocked my head back.

It hit the window behind me. I paused, then began slamming my head back repeatedly, rattling the glass.

Zen was beside me an instant later, grabbing me

roughly by the shoulder and towing me away from the building. She glanced in the window – apparently saw nobody there – then threw me to the ground.

'I am not a patient woman, Mister Leeds,' she said softly.

I was tempted to give her the drive right then. But I held back, suppressing my worry, and my fear.

Stall. Just a little bit more. 'You realize this is all pointless,' I lied to her. 'Panos already gave the information away. On the internet. Free, for everyone.'

She sniffed. 'We know that I3 contained his attempts to do that.'

He did? And … they did?

She pressed the gun down into my gut. Behind her, the window slammed open.

'Leeds!' the security guard shouted. 'You crazy man! Do you *want* to die? Because I'm going to strangle you … Hey! What's up?'

Zen met my eyes, then threw herself off me and dashed away around the corner. I leaned back as the security guard cursed, stretching out the window. 'Was that a gun she was carrying? Damn it, Leeds! What are you doing?'

'Surviving,' I said, tired, looking at my aspects. 'Move?'

'Now,' J.C. said.

We left the shouting guard and made for my car. I

scooped up my gun as I passed, and once out in the open, I didn't spot any sign of Zen. I climbed in the back of the vehicle and told Wilson to go.

I didn't feel much safer when we were on the road.

'I can't believe she tried that,' Ivy said. 'Practically in the open, without much proof that we even had what she wanted.'

'She was likely told to bring us in,' J.C. said. 'She's a professional; she wouldn't have moved this recklessly without external pressure. She reported to her superiors we might have something, then was told to recover it.'

I nodded, breathing in and out in deep, desperate breaths.

'Tobias,' Ivy said, taking over for me. 'What do we know about Exeltec?'

'Yol's report included some basic facts,' Tobias said. 'Biotech company much like I3, but far more … energetic, you might say. Founded five years ago, they soon released their key product – a pharmaceutical to help regulate the symptoms of Parkinson's disease.

'Unfortunately for them, a year later a rival company produced a much better alternative. Exeltec's product tanked. The company is owned by ten investors, with the largest stakeholder – the one Stephen imitated on the phone – acting as CEO and president of the board. Together they stand to lose a great deal of money on this company. Their last three products have flopped, and they are under investigation for cutting corners in overseas manufacturing. So, in a word, they're desperate.'

I nodded, calmed by Tobias's voice. I plugged the flash drive into my laptop, then started the footage at 10x speed and set the machine on the floor so I could watch it with half an eye. Tobias, often the most observant of my aspects, leaned down to watch in detail.

In the front seat, Wilson and Dion began chatting about the youth's home life. I felt the tremors from being held at gunpoint finally fade, and took stock. Wilson pulled onto the freeway; he wasn't going anywhere specific, but knew me well enough to realize I needed time to put myself together before giving him any specific directions.

Dion glanced in the rearview mirror to get a look at me. He caught me looking back at him and blushed, then slumped down into his seat, answering Wilson's questions about school. Dion had just finished high school, and was prepping for college in the fall. He readily answered Wilson's questions; it was difficult to resist the affable butler. Wilson could handle me, after all. Compared to that, normal people were easy.

'That must have been some event,' Wilson said to the young man, in response to an explanation of a recent race. 'Now, if you'll forgive the interruption, I should ask

Master Leeds where it was he wanted to be going.'

'You don't know already?' Dion asked, looking confused. 'But where have we been driving?'

'Around,' I said. 'I needed time to think. Dion, your brother lived with you and your mother, right?'

'Yeah. You know Greek families …'

I frowned. 'Not sure I do.'

'We're a tight lot,' Dion said with a shrug. 'Moving out on your own … well, that's just not done. Hell, I assume Panos would have stayed nearby even after he'd married. There's no resisting the pull of a Greek family.'

The key to Panos's corpse might very well be at the family home. At the very least, going there would indicate to Zen that we were still looking for something, which might encourage her to postpone another confrontation.

'Let's head there, Wilson,' I said. 'I want to talk to the family.'

'I *am* the family!' Dion said.

'The rest of the family,' I said, getting out my phone and dialing. 'Hold on a minute.' The phone rang a few times before being picked up.

'Yo, dawg,' Yol said.

'I don't think that's a cool phrase any longer, Yol.'

'I'm bringing it back, dawg.'

'I don't … You know what, never mind. I'm pretty sure

our bad guys are Exeltec.'

'Hmmm. That's unfortunate. I was hoping it was one of the other two. Let me step out so we can talk.'

'I wasn't certain they'd even let you answer while on lockdown.'

'It's a pain,' he said, and I heard the sound of a door closing, 'but I've managed a little freedom, since I'm not technically under arrest, I'm just quarantined. The feds let me set up a mobile office here, but nobody can get in or out until we convince them this thing wasn't contagious.'

'At least you can talk.'

'To an extent. It's a pain, dawg. How am I going to do press interviews for the new album?'

'Seclusion will just add to your celebrity mystique,' I said. 'Can you tell me anything more about Exeltec.'

'It's all in the documents I sent,' he explained. 'They're … well, they're bad news. I had a hunch it would be them. We've caught them trying to slip in spies in the form of engineers seeking employment.'

'Yol, they've got a hit man working for them.'

'That one you mentioned before?'

'Yeah. Ambushed me in an alley. Held me at gunpoint.'

Damn.

'I'm not going to sit around and let something like that happen again,' I said. 'I'm going to email you a list of instructions.'

'Instructions?' Yol asked. 'For what?'

'For keeping me from being killed,' I said, taking my laptop from Tobias. 'Yol, I have to ask you. What is it you're not telling me about this case?'

The line was silent.

'Yol ...'

'We didn't kill him,' Yol said. 'I promise you that.'

'But you *were* having him watched,' I said. 'You had his computer monitored. There's no other way you'd just naturally have a record of all of the things he'd been doing in the last few months, ready to print out when I arrived.'

'Yeah,' Yol admitted.

'And he was trying to give your information away,' I said. 'Post everything about the project online.'

In the front seat, Dion had turned around and was watching me.

'Some of the engineers didn't like me getting involved,' Yol said. 'They saw it as selling out. Panos ... that guy didn't believe in consequences. He'd have posted our research for everyone, so that every terrorist out there knew about it. I don't get such people, with their wikileaks and their open sources.'

'You're making it very hard for me to believe,' I said, 'that you didn't just remove him.'

Dion paled.

'I don't do things like that,' Yol snapped. 'Do you know how much a murder investigation can cost a company?'

I really wished I could trust him. To an extent, I *needed* to. Otherwise, I could very easily end this mission as a corpse myself. 'Just follow the instructions in my email,' I told him, then hung up.

I ignored Dion and began typing an email while the feed from the security camera continued to play on the other side of my laptop screen. Audrey stood up behind my seat and looked over my shoulder, watching me type.

'You shouldn't be out of your seat belt,' Ivy said.

'If we wreck, I'm sure Steve-O will imagine some delightfully gruesome scars for me,' Audrey said, then pointed at what I was typing. 'Rumors to be spread? About Exeltec? This will make them even *more* desperate.'

'I'm counting on it,' I said.

'Which will put an even bigger target on our heads!' Audrey said. 'What in the world are you planning?'

I didn't answer her, instead finishing up the instructions and shooting off the email to Yol. 'Dion,' I said, still half-watching the video on the laptop. 'Is your family religious?'

'My mom is,' he said from the front seat. 'I'm an atheist.' He said it stubbornly, as if this were something he'd had to defend in the past.

'Panos?'

'Atheist,' Dion said. 'Mom refused to accept it, of course.'

'Who's your family priest?'

'Father Frangos,' he said. 'Why?'

'Because I think someone impersonated him last night when visiting your brother's remains. Either that, or Father Frangos is involved in the theft of the corpse.'

Dion snorted. 'He's, like, ninety years old. He's so pious, when my mother told him I was taking after my brother, he fasted for thirty-six hours to pray for me. *Thirty-six* hours. I think the idea of intentionally breaking one of the commandments would kill him on the spot.'

The kid seemed to have gotten over his fear of me. Good.

'Ask him what he thought of his brother,' Ivy said from the back seat.

'Seems he liked the guy,' J.C. said with a grunt.

'Really?' Ivy said to him. 'You deduced that all on your own, did you? Steve, I'd like to hear an opinion of Panos that didn't come through Yol's channels. Get the kid talking, if you please.'

'Your brother,' I said to Dion. 'You seem to really dislike the company he was working for.'

'It used to be all right,' Dion said. 'Before it went and got all corporate. That's when the lies started, the extortion. It became about money.'

'Unlike other jobs,' Audrey said, 'which are never, ever about money.'

'Your brother continued working there,' I said to Dion, ignoring Audrey's commentary. 'So he couldn't have been too torn up about the changes at I3. I expect he wanted in on a little of that cash.'

Dion twisted around in his seat and fixed me with a glare that could have fried an egg. 'Panos cared *nothing* for the money. He only stayed at that place because of their resources.'

'So ... he needed I3's equipment,' I said. 'And, by extension, their money.'

'Yeah, well, it wasn't *about* the money. My brother was going to do great things. Cure diseases. He did things that even the others, traitors though they were, didn't know about. He –' Dion cut off, then turned around immediately in his seat, and refused to respond to further prodding.

I looked at Ivy.

'Serious hero worship going on there,' she said, 'I suspect that if you prodded, you'd find Dion was planning to study biology and follow in his brother's footsteps. The philosophy, the mannerisms ... We can learn a lot about

Panos by watching his brother.'

'So,' J.C. said, 'you're telling me Panos was an annoying little sh—'

'Anyway,' Ivy interrupted, 'if it's true that Panos was working on projects even Garvas and the others didn't know about, that could be the true secret Yol is trying to recover.'

I nodded.

'Stephen,' Tobias said, pointing at the laptop screen. 'You'll want to watch this.'

I leaned over, then rewound the footage. Tobias, Audrey, and J.C. huddled around, all ignoring Ivy's pointed complaints that none of us were bothering with seat belts. On the small screen, now playing at normal speed, I watched someone leave the bathroom in the medical complex.

The cleaning lady. She pulled a large trash can on wheels, and approached the doorway into the coroner's offices, then opened the door and went in.

'Does *nobody* in this world care about security anymore?' J.C. said, pointing at the screen. 'Look at the security guard! He's didn't even *glance* at her.'

I froze the frame. The camera was positioned in such a way that we couldn't get a good look at the figure, even when I rewound and froze it again.

'Somewhat small in stature,' Tobias said. 'Dark-haired,

female. I can't pick out anything else. The rest of you?'

J.C. and Audrey shook their heads. I froze the frame on the security guard. It was a different man from the one we'd met, a smaller fellow, who was sitting in the station and reading a paperback novel. I rewound to try to find where the cleaning lady entered the building, but she must have come in the back. I did catch the security guard pushing a button, perhaps to open the back door for someone who had buzzed for the lock to open.

Fast-forwarding, we watched the cleaning lady leave the coroner's offices and go into each room along the hall. Whoever it was, she knew not to break pattern. She cleaned the other offices quickly, then disappeared down the hallway, towing her large trash can.

'That trash can could most certainly hide a body,' J.C. said. 'I thought the guard said nobody went into those rooms!'

'Cleaning staff is usually considered "nobody",' Tobias observed. 'And the door into the morgue itself would be locked. Liza said even the security guard wouldn't be able to get in, so presumably the cleaning staff doesn't go into that room, at least not without supervision.'

'Does that drive have footage from other nights?' Audrey asked.

'Good idea,' I said, searching and finding the two previous nights' footage as well. We watched, and found that at around the same time each night, a cleaning person entered and engaged in a similar activity. But the trash can they brought was smaller, and it was obviously a different person. Female, yes, and with a similar build – but with lighter hair.

'So,' Audrey said, 'they replaced first the priest and then the cleaning lady.'

'This should have been impossible,' J.C. said. 'Protocol should have made it so.'

'And what protocol is that?' Audrey said. 'This isn't a high-security facility, J.C. You spend year after year without any kind of incident, and of course you're going to grow lax. Besides, the people who pulled this off were capable. Fake ID, knowledge of the times the cleaning lady entered and left. The uniform is the same, and they even cleaned the entire set of offices so nobody would be suspicious.'

I replayed the footage of the thief, wondering if it was Zen herself. The build was right. What was it Audrey had said before? People are usually far less secure than the encryption strategies – or, in this case, security devices – they employ. This could have all been stopped if the guard had glanced at the cleaning lady. But he didn't, and why would he have? What was there *really* in these offices that someone would want to steal?

Just a corpse carrying a doomsday weapon.

I stifled a yawn as we eventually pulled into a residential area. Blast. I'd been hoping to find a chance to squeeze in a nap while we were driving. Even thirty minutes would do me some good. No chance for that now. Instead, I replied to Yol's return email, telling him that yes, I did want to make Exeltec more frantic, and yes, I did know what I was doing. My next set of instructions seemed to placate him.

We pulled up to a quaint white suburban house, rambler style, with a neatly mowed lawn and vines growing up the walls. A careful air of cultivation helped offset the fact that this house – with its siding, its small windows, and its lack of an enclosed garage – was probably a decade or four past its prime.

'You're not going to hurt my family, are you?' Dion asked from the front seat.

'No,' I said, 'but I might embarrass you a little.'

Dion grunted.

'Come introduce me,' I said, shoving open the door. 'We're on the same side. I promise that when I recover your brother's body, I won't let I3 do anything nefarious with it. In fact, I'll let you watch the cremation – with I3 getting no chance to lay hands on the body – if you want.'

Dion sighed, but joined me in climbing from the car

14

'Keep watch,' I said to J.C. as we approached the house. 'I haven't forgotten that Zen is out there.'

'We might want to call in some backup,' J.C. said.

'More Rescue Rangers?' Ivy asked.

'*Time* Rangers,' J.C. snapped. 'And no, we don't have temporal substance here. I was talking about real body-guards. If Skinny hired a few of those, I'd feel a whole lot safer.'

I shook my head. 'No time, unfortunately.'

'Perhaps you should have explained the truth to Zen,' Tobias said, jogging up. 'Was it wise to let her think we have the information she wants?'

Behind us, Wilson pulled the SUV away – I'd given him instructions to keep driving until I called him for a pickup. I didn't want Zen deciding to apply a little interrogation to my servant. Unfortunately, if she was determined, simply driving away wouldn't be enough to protect him. Perhaps I *should* have told Zen we didn't have her information. Yet my instincts said that the less she knew about what I'd discovered, the better off I'd be. I just needed to have a plan in place to deal with her.

Dion led us up to the house, glanced over his shoulder at me, then sighed and pushed open the door. I grabbed it and held it for my aspects, then slipped in last.

The house smelled old. Of furniture that had been polished over and over, of stale potpourri, and of burned wood from an old hearth. The careful clutter offered a new oddity on each wall and surface – a line of photos in novelty frames down one hallway, a collection of ceramic cats in a shadow box near the door, a sequence of colorful candles on the mantel with a religious tone to them. The house didn't look lived in, it looked decorated. This was a museum for a family's life, and they'd done a lot of living.

Dion hung his coat beside the door. The only coat there; the rest were stored neatly inside an open coat closet. He walked down the hallway, calling for his mother.

I lingered, stepping into the living room, with its rug on top of carpet and its easy chair with worn armrests. My aspects fanned out. I stepped up beside the hearth, inspecting a beautiful wall cross made from glass.

'Catholic?' I asked, noticing Ivy's reverence.

'Close,' she said. 'Greek Orthodox. That's a depiction of Emperor Constantine.'

'Very religious,' I said, noting the candles, the paintings, the cross.

'Or just very fond of decoration,' she said. 'What are we looking for?'

'The decryption code,' I said, turning. 'Audrey? Any idea what it might look like.'

'It's digital,' she said. 'For a one-time pad, the key is going to be as long as the data being stored. That's why Zen was after the flash drive.'

I looked around the room. With all of this stuff, a flash drive could be hidden practically anywhere. Tobias, Audrey, and J.C. started looking. Ivy remained beside me.

'Needle in a haystack?' I asked her softly.

'Possibly,' she said, folding her arms, tapping one finger against the opposite forearm. 'Let's go look at pictures of the family. Maybe we can determine something from them.'

I nodded, walking over to the hallway that led to the kitchen, where I'd spotted pictures of the family. Four in a row were formal photos of each member of the family. The picture of the father was old, from the seventies; he'd died when the boys were children. The mother's picture and Dion's picture had what appeared to be pictures of saints hanging beneath them.

No saint beneath Panos. 'A symbol that he'd given up on his faith?' I asked, pointing to the empty spot.

'Nothing so dramatic,' Ivy said. 'When a member of the Greek Orthodox Church is buried, a picture of Christ or their patron saint is buried with them. That picture would have been taken down in preparation for his funeral.'

I nodded, walking on a little further, searching for pictures of the family interacting. I paused beside one that showed a smiling Panos from not too long ago. He was holding up a fish while his mother – in sunglasses – hugged him from the side.

'Open and friendly, by all accounts,' Ivy said. 'An idealist who joined with friends from college to start their own company. "If this works," he wrote on a forum a few months back, "then any person in any country could have access to powerful computing. Their own body supplies the energy, the storage, even the processing." Others on the forum warned about the dangers of wetware. Panos argued with them. He saw all of this as some kind of information revolution, a step forward for humankind.'

'Is there anything about those posts of his that doesn't add up?'

'Ask Audrey about that,' Ivy said. 'I'm focused on Panos

the man. Who was he? How would he act?'

'He was working on something,' I said. 'Curing diseases, is that what Dion said? I'll bet he was really annoyed when the others pulled him off of his virus research because of the cancer scare.'

'Yol knows that Panos got further in his research than he let on. It's clear to me. Yol was spying on Panos and is really, really worried about all of this. That implies he's worried about a danger even more catastrophic than their little cancer scare. That's why Yol brought you in, and why he's so desperate for you to destroy the body.'

I nodded slowly. 'So what about Panos? What can you guess about him and the key?'

'If he even used one,' Ivy said, 'I suspect he'd give it to a family member.'

'Agreed,' I said as Dion finally headed out the back doors, calling for his mother in the backyard.

I felt a moment of concern. Had Zen been here before us? But no. Stepping into the kitchen, I was able to see the mother outside pruning a tree. Dion walked out to her.

I delayed a moment, stepping up to Audrey and J.C.

'So,' Audrey was saying, 'in the future, do we have flying cars?'

'I'm not from *your* future,' J.C. said. 'I'm from a parallel dimension, and you're from another one.'

'And does yours have flying cars?'

'That's classified,' J.C. said. 'So far as I can tell you, my dimension is basically like this one – only, I exist there.'

'In other words, that one is way, *way* worse.'

'I should shoot you, woman.'

'Try it.'

I stopped between them, but J.C. just grunted. 'Don't tempt me,' he growled at Audrey.

'No, really,' Audrey said. 'Shoot me. Go ahead. Then, when it doesn't do anything because we're both *imaginary*, you'll have to admit the truth: That you're crazy, even for a figment of a deranged man's psyche. That he imagined you as a repository for information. That, in truth, you're just a flash drive yourself, J.C.'

He glared at her, then stalked away, head down.

'And,' Audrey shouted after him, 'you –'

I took her by the arm. 'Enough.'

'It's good for someone to bring him down a notch or two, Steve-O,' she said. 'Can't have pieces of your brain getting too uppity, can we?'

'What about you?'

'I'm different,' she said.

'Oh? And you'd be fine if I just stopped imagining you?'

'You don't know how to do that,' she said, uncomfortably.

'I'm pretty sure that if J.C. *did* shoot you, my mind would follow through accordingly. You'd die, Audrey. So be careful what you ask for.'

She glanced to the side, then shuffled from one foot to the other. 'So … uh … what did you want?'

'You're the closest thing I've got to a data analyst right now,' I said. 'The information that Yol gave us. Think about the emails, forum posts, and personal information from Panos's computer. I need to know what he isn't saying.'

'What he *isn't* saying?'

'What's hidden, Audrey. Inconsistencies. Clues. I need to know what he was really working on – his secret projects. There's a good chance he hinted at this online somewhere.'

'Okay … I'll think about it.' She'd gone from a niche expertise – handwriting analysis – to something broader. Hopefully this was the start of a trend. I was running out of space for aspects; it was getting harder and harder to contain them, manage them, imagine them all at once. I suspected that was why Audrey had insisted on coming on this mission – deep down, part of me knew that I needed my aspects to begin doubling up on skills.

She looked at me, eyes focusing. 'Actually, as I consider it, I might have something for you right now. Viruses.'

'What about them?

'Panos spent a *lot* of time on immunology forums, talking about disease, getting into very technical discussions with people who study bacteria and viruses. None of what he said is revelatory, but when you look at the whole …'

'His history was in microbial gene splicing,' I said. 'Makes sense for him to be there.'

'But Garvas said they'd abandoned viruses as a method of data delivery,' Audrey said. 'However, Panos's forum posts on these subjects *increased* once I3 abandoned that part of the project.' She looked at me, then grinned. 'I figured that out!'

'Nice.'

'Well, I mean, I guess *you* figured that out.' She folded her arms. 'Being an imaginary person makes it difficult to feel any real sense of accomplishment.'

'Just imagine your sense of accomplishment,' I said. 'You're imaginary, so imaginary accomplishment should work for you.'

'But if I'm imaginary, and I imagine something, it's *doubly* unreal. Like using a copy machine to copy something that's just been copied.'

'Actually,' Tobias said, strolling up, 'theoretically the imaginary sense of accomplishment would *have* to be imagined by the primary imaginer, so it wouldn't be an iteration as you suggest.'

'It doesn't work that way,' Audrey said. 'Trust me, I'm the expert on being imaginary.'

'But … If we are all aspects …'

'Yeah, but I'm *more* imaginary than you,' she said. 'Or, well, less. Since I know all about it.' She grinned at him, triumphant, as he rubbed his chin, trying to sort through that.

'You're crazy,' I said softly, looking at Audrey.

'Huh?'

It had just struck me. Audrey was insane.

Each of my aspects were. I barely noticed Tobias's schizophrenia anymore, let alone Ivy's trypophobia. But the madness was there, lurking. Each aspect had one, whether it be fear of germs, technophobia, or megalomania. I'd never realized what Audrey's was until now.

'You think you're imaginary,' I told her.

'Duh.'

'But it's not because you're actually imaginary. It's because you have a psychosis that makes you think you're imaginary. You'd think this even if you happened to be real.'

It was hard to see. Many of the aspects accepted their lot, but few confronted it. Even Ivy did that with difficulty. But Audrey flaunted it; she reveled in it. That was because, in her brain, she was a real person who was crazy and therefore thought she wasn't real. I'd assumed she was self-aware, but that wasn't it at all. She was as crazy as the others. Her insanity just happened to align with reality.

She glanced at me, then shrugged, and immediately tried to deflect the conversation by asking Tobias about the weather. He, of course, referenced his delusion who lived in the satellite far above. I shook my head, then turned.

And found Dion standing in the doorway, a distinctly uncomfortable look on his face. How much had he watched? He gave me a look like one might give an unfamiliar dog that had just been barking frantically but now seemed calm. Through that whole exchange, I'd been a crazy man, stalking around and talking to himself.

No. I'm not crazy. I have it under control.

Maybe that was my only real madness. Thinking I could handle all of this.

'You found your mother?' I asked.

'In the backyard,' Dion said, thumbing over his shoulder.

'Let's go talk to her,' I said, brushing past him.

15

I found Ivy and J.C. outside, sitting on the steps. She was rubbing his back as he sat with hands hanging before him, gun in one of them, staring at a beetle crossing the ground. Ivy gave me a glance and shook her head. Not a good time to talk to him.

I headed across the well-tended lawn with Audrey and Tobias in tow. Mrs. Maheras had finished pruning and was now inspecting her tomato plants, pulling off bugs, pulling weeds.

She didn't look up as I approached. 'Stephen Leeds,' she said. Her voice bore a distinct Greek accent. 'You're famous, I hear.'

'Only among people who like gossip,' I said, kneeling down. 'The tomatoes look nice. Growing well.'

'I started them inside,' she said, lifting one of the plump green fruits. 'Tomatoes do better after the late frosts are past, but I can't help wanting to get an early start.'

I waited for Ivy to give me a prompt on what to say, but she was still on the steps. *Idiot*, I thought at myself. 'So … you like to garden a lot?'

Mrs. Maheras looked up and met my eyes. 'I appreciate people who make decisions and act on them, Mister Leeds. Not people who try to make small talk about things in which they obviously have no interest.'

'Several pieces of me are very interested in gardening,' I said. 'I just didn't bring them along.'

She regarded me, waiting.

I sighed. 'Mrs. Maheras, what do you know of your son's research?'

'Almost nothing,' she said. 'Ghastly business.'

I frowned.

'She thinks it took him away from the church,' Dion said behind me, kicking at a clump of dirt. 'All of that science and questioning. Heaven help us if a man spends his time *thinking*.'

'Dion,' she said, 'don't speak stupidity.'

He folded his arms and met her gaze, defiant.

'You work for the people who employed my son,' Mrs. Maheras said, looking at me.

'I just want to find his body,' I said. 'Before anything dangerous happens. What can you tell me of your priest?'

'Father Frangos?' she asked. 'Why ever would you want to know about him?'

'He was the last person to see the body,' I said. 'He visited the coroner on the night before your son's corpse vanished.'

'Don't be silly,' Mrs. Maheras said. 'He did nothing of the sort – he was here. I requested a house blessing, and he visited.'

To the side, Tobias and Audrey shared a glance. So we had a witness that Father Frangos had *not* gone in to see the body. Proof an impostor was involved. But what good did that knowledge do us?

'Did Panos give you anything, before he passed away?' I asked her.

'No.'

'It might have been something trivial,' I said. 'Are you sure? There's nothing you can think of?'

She turned back to her plants. 'No.'

'Did he spend time with anyone in particular during the last few months?'

'Just the men from that ghastly laboratory.'

I knelt beside her. 'Mrs. Maheras,' I said softly. 'Lives are at stake because of your son's research. Many lives. If you are hiding something, you could well cause a national disaster. You don't need to give it to me. The police – or, better, the FBI – would work just fine. Just don't gamble with this. Please.'

She glanced at me, lips pursed. Then, her expression hardened. 'I have nothing for you.'

I sighed and rose. 'Thank you.' I walked away from her, back toward the steps, where J.C. had perked up a little at Ivy's prodding.

'Well?' he asked me.

'Stonewalled,' I said. 'If he did give the key to her, she wouldn't tell me.'

'Coming here was a mistake,' J.C. said. 'A distraction from what we need to do.'

I glanced at the mother, who had continued to regard me, trowel in her hand.

'Admit it, Skinny,' J.C. continued. 'If we don't do something soon, the world is going to get cancer.' He hesitated. 'Smet, it sounds stupid when I say it like that.'

'… "Smet"?' I asked.

'Future curse.'

'Why does it sound so much like –'

'Future curses *always* sound like our curses,' J.C. said, rolling his eyes. 'But they're not, so it's okay to say them when prudes are around.' He thumbed at Ivy, still sitting beside him.

'Wait,' Ivy said. 'I thought you were from another dimension, not from the future.'

'Nonsense. I've always been from the future.'

'Since when?'

'Since two days from now,' J.C. said. 'Look, Skinny, do I need to repeat myself? You know what our next move is.'

I sighed, then nodded. 'Yes. It's time to break into Exeltec.'

PART 3

16

'Are you *sure* about this?' Ivy said, rushing along beside me as I strode out of the front of the house.

'It's our best lead, Ivy,' J.C. said. 'We don't have time to investigate new threads. Exeltec has the body. We need to find out where it is and steal it back from them.'

I nodded. 'Panos's key could be almost anywhere, but if we destroy the corpse, then the key doesn't matter.' I raised my phone, noticing that I'd missed a call from Yol. I nodded for J.C. to watch the perimeter as I texted Wilson for a pick-up, then dialed Yol back.

Yol picked up the line.

'Hey,' I said. 'I –'

'I don't have much time,' Yol interrupted, voice muffled. 'This is bad, Legion. *Seriously* bad.'

I grew cold. 'What happened?'

'Panos,' Yol said, talking quickly, his accent growing

thicker in his haste. 'He let something out. Damn it. It's –'
He cut off.

'Yol?' I said, growing tense as Ivy and Tobias crowded
in, trying to hear what was being said. 'Yol!'

I heard voices on the other end of the line, followed
by rasping. 'I'm being arrested,' Yol said a moment later.
'No more information in or out. They're going to take
my phone.'

'What did Panos let out, Yol?' I asked.

'We don't know. The feds tripped a hidden file on his
computer. It erased the damn thing and popped up a
screen that taunted us, saying he'd already released his
infection. They're freaking out. I don't know anything
else.'

'And the things I asked you to do?'

'Did some. Set others in motion. Don't know if I'll be
able to finish.'

'Yol, my life could depend on whether or not –'

'*All* of our lives are in danger,' Yol snapped. 'Didn't you
hear me? This is a disaster. Hell! They're here. Find that
body. Find out *what that man did*!'

The phone rustled again, and the line went dead. I had
the distinct impression that Yol hadn't hung up – someone
had taken the phone from him. The feds now likely knew
I was involved.

I lowered the phone and looked at my aspects as Wilson pulled up. Behind us, Dion trailed out of the house, hands in his pockets. He looked troubled.

'We need to get moving,' J.C. said, rushing back from watching the perimeter. 'Zen could show up here at any moment.'

'If she does,' I said, 'Mrs. Maheras is in danger. I'm surprised Zen hasn't been here already – if not her, then another Exeltec flunky.' I frowned. 'I feel like we're a step behind. I do *not* like that sensation.'

I ignored the car waiting for us, and I barely noticed Dion as he walked up. Instead, I closed my eyes. 'Tobias,' I whispered.

'Have you noticed the beauty of the landscaping here?' Tobias said. 'Those are tuberous begonia, challenging flowers to raise, particularly in this region. They require lots of light, but it can't be direct, and are very sensitive to frost. Ah, I remember a story about them ...'

He talked on. The other aspects fell silent as we thought, collectively. I would not proceed, feeling I'd missed something. Something that one of us should have spotted. What was it?

'Zen,' J.C. interrupted suddenly. 'Her ambush.'

'People are far less secure,' I whispered, opening my eyes, 'than their security measures.' I reached up to my shoulder, where Zen had grabbed me in the alleyway to pull me away from the building, then I moved up to touch under my shirt collar.

My fingers brushed metal.

'Oh, *holy hell!*' J.C. said.

Zen had bugged me. *That* was what the attack in the alleyway had been about. It hadn't been nearly as reckless as she'd made it seem. My mind raced as J.C. explained to the other aspects what had happened. What had I said out loud? What did Zen know?

She'd heard that I intended to break into Exeltec. But what about the instructions I'd sent Yol? Did she know about those?

Sweating, I traced back through my memory. No. I'd only written that information down in the email. But she did know what I'd said to Mrs. Maheras. She knew that I was at a dead end.

'I'm an idiot,' J.C. said. 'We thought to have you scrub down after the restaurant, but not after actual *physical contact* with the assassin?'

'She hid her intentions well,' Audrey replied. 'Masked it as a frantic attempt to get the flash drive.'

'At least now we probably don't have to worry about her coming to hurt Mrs. Maheras.'

Probably. I stared at my phone. How had we missed this?

'Calm, Stephen,' Tobias said, resting a hand on my shoulder. 'Everyone makes mistakes, even you. We can use this one – the assassin is listening to us, but she doesn't know you've figured that out. We can manipulate her.'

I nodded, taking a deep breath. Zen knew about the plan to infiltrate Exeltec, which meant I couldn't go through with that. I needed something new, something better.

That meant relying on the things I'd set in motion with Yol. Making Exeltec's owners frantic, then playing upon that. Why did missions always go this way, lately? I looked up at my aspects, then made the decision, punching a number on my phone.

Someone picked up. 'Oh, honey,' a sultry voice said on the other end of the line, 'I was *hoping* you'd call me today.'

'Bianca,' I said.

Tobias groaned. 'Not *her*.'

I ignored him. 'I need information,' I said to the woman on the line.

'Sure thing, sugar,' she said. How *did* she purr like that? I was half-convinced she used some kind of sound effect machine. 'What about? Your … date the other night? I can tell you the names of the people who set you up.'

'It's not about that,' I said. 'There's something going on with a company called I3 and their rival, Exeltec. I think they might have released a deadly virus into the wild. Do you know anything about it?'

'Mmm … I can look,' Bianca said. 'Might take some time.'

'Anything you can get me on Exeltec would be heartily appreciated,' I said.

'Sure,' she said. 'And honey, next time you need a date, why not give me a call? I'm *so offended* that I wasn't even considered!'

'Like you'd show,' I said. Three years, and I'd never seen Bianca face-to-face.

'I'd at least contemplate it,' she said. 'Now, you've got to give me *something* for the newspapers. About your date?'

'Get me information on Exeltec,' I said, 'and we'll trade.' I hung up, looking over my shoulder as Dion stepped up to me on the sidewalk, looking confused.

'What are you hoping to find out?' the kid asked.

'Nothing,' I replied, fully aware that Zen was listening to all this. 'Bianca is a *terrible* informant. I've never gotten a drop of useful information out of her, and after I call her, most of what I say ends up on the internet within minutes.'

'But –'

I dialed another informant and initiated a similar, but more circumspect, line of inquiry. Then a third. Within a few minutes I'd ensured that very, very soon everyone who cared about Exeltec would be reading about how they'd been involved in a major public safety breach. With I3 being investigated and me being involved, the kernel of truth to the rumors I'd started would set off a media frenzy.

'You're pushing them up against the wall, Steve,' Ivy said as Wilson finally pulled up. 'Zen's employers were desperate before; they'll be *rabid* once this hits.'

'Hoping to make them ignore you and focus on damage control with the media?' J.C. asked. 'Not smart. Whipping the tiger won't distract it; the thing will just get angrier.'

I couldn't explain, not with Zen listening. Instead, I got out my note pad and scribbled a few instructions to Wilson, assuming the aspects would see and catch on.

Surprisingly, Audrey seemed to get it first. She grinned. 'Oooh …'

'Dangerous,' Ivy said, folding her arms. '*Very* dangerous.'

Wilson rolled down the passenger window. 'Master Leeds?'

I finished writing and leaned in through the window, handing him the message. 'Some instructions,' I said. 'I need you to stay here, Wilson, and watch Mrs. Maheras. I'm worried the assassin might try to get to her. In fact, you should probably get her to the nearest police station.'

'But who will drive you?'

'I can drive,' I said.

Wilson looked skeptical.

'Funny,' Audrey remarked, 'how a man can trust you to save the world, but not to feed or drive yourself.'

I smiled reassuringly at Wilson as he looked down at the instructions in his hand, then back at me with a worried expression.

'Please,' I said to him.

Wilson sighed and nodded, climbing out of the car.

'You coming?' I said to Dion as I opened the side door of the SUV for my aspects and let them pile in.

'You said that people could be in danger,' Dion said.

'They are,' I replied, closing the door behind Audrey. 'What your brother let out could cost the lives of millions.'

'He said it wasn't dangerous,' Dion said stubbornly.

Damn. The kid was holding out on me. Did *he* have the key? Unfortunately, I didn't want him to talk and let Zen hear. Well, either way, I needed him with me. I might need an extra pair of nonimaginary hands, now that I'd sent Wilson away.

I settled into the driver's seat, and Dion climbed into the front passenger seat. 'Panos didn't do anything wrong.'

'And what *did* he do?' I asked, resigned. If I didn't prod, it would look suspicious to Zen.

'Something,' Dion said.

'How pleasantly descriptive.'

'He wouldn't tell me. I don't think he even actually finished it. But it wasn't dangerous.'

'I …' I trailed off, looking back as J.C.'s mobile phone went off. The ring tone was 'America the Beautiful.' I shook my head, starting the car and pulling away – leaving an overwhelmed-looking Wilson on the curb – as J.C. answered his phone.

'Yo, Achmed,' he said. 'Yeah, I've got him here. Video? I can do that. Hey, you gonna fix that Chinese stuff for us again?'

'It was *Indian* food,' Kalyani said, now on speaker. 'Why would you assume it's Chinese?'

'Had rice, didn't it?' J.C. said, kneeling beside the armrest between driver's seat and passenger, then holding the phone out for me.

'Coconut rice, and curry, and … Never mind. Mister Steve?'

'Yeah?' I said, glancing at the phone. Kalyani waved happily, wearing a simple T-shirt and jeans. Her bindi was black today and shaped like a little arrow between her eyebrows, rather than being the traditional red dot. I'd have to ask her about the significance.

'We've been talking,' Kalyani said. 'And Arnaud wants

to tell you something.' She turned the phone to the punctilious little Frenchman. He leaned forward, blinking at the screen. I kept my time divided between him and the road.

'Monsieur,' Arnaud said, 'I have spoken with Clive and Mi Won. The three of us, you see, had some upper-level chemistry and biology courses as part of our schooling. We cannot dig too deeply, because … Well, you know.'

'I do.' Ignacio. His death had ripped away most of my knowledge of chemistry.

'Regardless,' Arnaud said, 'we have been pouring over the information given to us. Mi Won is insistent, and we have come to agree with her. It is our admittedly amateur opinion that I3 and the man named Yol are lying to you.'

'About what specifically?'

'About giving up on a viral delivery method into the body,' Arnaud said. 'Monsieur, Panos had too many resources – was progressing too well – on his supposedly "secret" project to have been cut off. They were investigating that line, no matter what they told you. In addition, we are not convinced that this cancer threat is as viable as it first seemed. Oh, that is *theoretically* where this research could lead, but from what we've gathered from the notes, I3 had not reached such a point yet.'

'So they didn't want to tell me what the real crisis was,'

I said. 'The rogue bacteria or virus that Panos spliced, whatever it is.'

'That is for you to consider,' Arnaud said. 'We are scientists. All we are saying is that there are layers here beyond what we are being told.'

'Thank you,' I said. 'I suspected, but this confirmation is helpful. Is that everything?'

'One more item,' Kalyani said, taking back the phone and turning it around toward her smiling face. 'I wanted to introduce to you my husband, Rahul.' An Indian man with a round, mustached face stepped into view beside her, then waved at me.

I felt a chill.

'I told you that he is a good photographer,' Kalyani said, 'but you do not need to use him that way. He is a *very* clever man. He can do all sorts of things! He knows computers well.'

'I can see him,' I said. 'Why can I see him?'

'He's joined us!' Kalyani said, excited. 'Isn't it wonderful!'

'Very pleased to meet you, Mister Stephen,' Rahul said with a melodic Indian accent. 'I will be very helpful, I can promise you.'

'I …' I swallowed. 'How … did you …'

'This is bad,' Ivy said from the back seat. 'Have you ever manifested an aspect unintentionally?'

'Not since the early days,' I whispered. 'And never without researching a new topic first.'

'Man,' Audrey said. 'Kalyani gets a husband and I can't even have a gerbil? Totally unfair.'

I pulled over immediately, not caring about the car that honked beside me as I swerved. As we lurched to a stop I yanked the phone from J.C.'s hand and stared at the new aspect. This was the first time any family member of one of my delusions had appeared to me. It seemed a very dangerous precedent. Another sign that I was losing control.

I hung up, making their smiling faces wink out, then tossed the phone over my shoulder to J.C. Sweating, I pulled the car forward, earning a honk from another car. I took the first off-ramp I saw, veering down into the city.

'You okay?' Dion asked.

'Fine,' I snapped.

I needed a place to go, a place to think. A place that would look natural, but where I could stall and wait for my plan to proceed without Zen getting suspicious. I pulled into a Denny's. 'Just need some food,' I lied. This would work, right? Even a man trying to save the world had to eat.

Dion glanced at me. 'You sure you're –'

'Yes. I just need an omelet.'

17

I held the restaurant door for my aspects, then walked in after them. The place smelled of coffee, and was occupied by the late-morning breakfast crowd, which was perfect. Zen was less likely to try something with so many witnesses. It took some work to get the waitress to give us a table for six; I had to lie and say we were expecting more people. Eventually, we settled down, Dion opposite me and two aspects on either side.

I held up a menu, fingers sticking to syrup on one side, but didn't read. Instead, I tried to calm my breathing. Sandra hadn't prepared me for this. The family members of aspects appearing suddenly, without research being done?

'You're crazy,' a voice whispered across from me. 'Like … *actually* crazy.'

I lowered my menu which – I only now realized – I'd been holding upside down. The kid hadn't touched his.

'No I'm not,' I said. 'I'll give you, I might be a touch insane. But I'm *not* crazy.'

'They're the same thing.'

'From your perspective, perhaps,' I said. 'I see it differently – but even if we admit that the word applies to me, it applies to you too. The longer I've lived, the more I've realized everyone is neurotic in their own individual way. *I* have control of my psychoses. How about you?'

Beside me, Ivy sniffed at my use of the word 'control'.

Dion chewed on this, leaning back in his chair. 'What do they say my brother did?'

'He claims to have released something. A virus or bacteria of some sort.'

'He wouldn't have done that,' Dion said immediately. 'He wanted to help people. It was the others that were dangerous. They wanted to make weapons.'

'He told you this?'

'Well, no,' Dion admitted. 'But, I mean, why else would they try to force him to give up his projects? Why would they watch him so closely? You should be investigating *them*, not my brother. Their secrets are the dangerous ones.'

'Typical pseudo-intellectual teen liberal prattle,' J.C. said from my right, looking over his menu. 'I'll have the steak and eggs. Rare and runny.'

I nodded absently as the others spoke up. At the very

least, the server wouldn't have reason to complain about us taking up so many seats – seeing as how I'd be ordering five meals. Part of me wished I could have them give the meals to others after I was done imagining my aspects cleaning their plates.

I turned my attention to the menu, and found I wasn't that hungry. I ordered an omelet anyway, talking to the waitress as the kid dug in his pocket, obviously determined not to let me pay for him. He came out with a few wadded-up bills and ordered a breakfast burrito.

I kept waiting for a beep from my phone, telling me that Wilson had followed my instructions. Nothing came, and I felt myself growing increasingly anxious; I wiped the sweat from my temples with my napkin. My aspects tried to relax me, Tobias chatting about the origin of the pancake as a food, Ivy engaging him and acting very interested.

'What's that?' I asked, nodding at Dion, who was staring at a little slip of paper he'd found among the wadded-up bills.

He blushed immediately, moving to tuck it away.

I snatched his hand, moving with reflexes I didn't know I had. Beside me, J.C. nodded appreciatively.

'It's nothing,' Dion snapped, opening his hand. 'Fine. Take it. Idiot.'

I suddenly felt foolish. Panos's data key wouldn't be a slip of paper; it would have to be on a flash drive or some other electronic storage medium. I pulled my hand back, reading the piece of paper. *1 Esd 4:41*, it read.

'Mom slips them into my pockets when she's folding laundry,' Dion explained. 'Reminders to give up my heathen ways.'

I showed it to the others, frowning. 'I don't recognize that scripture.'

'First Esdras,' Ivy said. 'From the Orthodox Bible – it's a book of Apocrypha that most other sects don't use. I don't know that particular verse offhand.'

I looked it up on my phone. 'Great is truth,' I read, 'and strongest of all.'

Dion shrugged. 'I suppose I can agree with that. Even if Mom won't accept what the truth really is …'

I tapped my finger on the table. I felt as if I was close to something. An answer? Or maybe just the right questions to be asking? 'Your brother had a data key,' I said, 'which would unlock the information stored in his body. Would he have given it to your mother, do you think?'

Ivy watched Dion carefully to see if he reacted to mention of the key. He didn't have any reaction I could see, and Ivy shook her head. If he was surprised we knew about the key, he was hiding it very well.

'A data key?' Dion asked. 'Like what?'

'A thumb drive or something similar.'

'I doubt he'd give anything like that to Mom,' Dion said as our food arrived. 'She hates technology and everything to do with it, particularly if she thinks it came from I3. If he'd handed her something like that, she'd have just destroyed it.'

'She gave me quite the cold reception.'

'Well, what did you expect? You're employed by the company that turned her son away from God.' Dion shook his head. 'Mom's a good person – solid, salt-of-the-earth, Old World stock. But she doesn't trust technology. To her, work is something you do with your hands. Not this idle staring at computer screens.' He looked away. 'I think Panos did what he did to prove something to her, you know?'

'Turning people into mass storage devices?' I asked.

Dion blushed. 'That's just the setup, the work he had to do in *order* to do the work he wanted.'

'Which was?'

'I …'

'Yeah,' Ivy said. 'He knows something here. Man, this kid is not good at lying. Take a dominant position, Steve. Push him.'

'Might as well tell me,' I said. 'Someone needs to know,

Dion. You don't know that you can trust me, but you have to tell someone. What *was* your brother trying to do?'

'Disease,' Dion said, looking at his burrito. 'He wanted to cure it.'

'Which one?'

'All of it.'

'Lofty goal.'

'Yeah, Panos admitted as much to me. The actual curing wasn't his job; he saw the delivery method as his part.'

'Delivery method?' I asked, frowning. 'Of the disease.'

'No. Of the cure.'

'Ahhh …' Tobias said, nodding as he sipped his coffee.

'Think about it,' Dion said, gesturing to the sides, animated. 'Infectious disease is pretty awesome. Imagine if we could design a fast-spreading virus which, in turn, *immunized* people from another disease? You catch the common cold, and suddenly you can never get smallpox, AIDS, polio … Why spend billions immunizing, trying to reach people? Nature itself could do all the work for us, if we cracked the method.'

'That sounds … incredible,' I said.

'Incredibly *terrifying*,' J.C. said, pointing at the kid with his knife. 'Sounds a little like using a smarkwat to fight a viqxuixs.'

'A what?' Ivy asked, sighing.

'Classified,' J.C. said. 'Smet, this steak is good.' He dug back into the food.

'Yeah, well,' Dion said. 'I was going to help him, you know? Go to school, eventually start a new biotech company with him. I guess that dream is dead too.' He stabbed at his food. 'But you know, each day he'd come home and Mom would ask, "Did you do any good today?" 'And he'd smile. He knew he was doing something important, even if she couldn't see it.'

'I suspect,' I said, 'that your mother was prouder of him than she let on.'

'Yeah, probably. She's not as bad as she seems sometimes. When we were younger, she worked long hours in menial jobs, supporting us after Dad died. I shouldn't complain. It's just ... you know, she thinks she knows *everything*.'

'Unlike your average teenager,' Audrey said, smiling toward Dion.

I nodded, toying with my food, watching Dion. 'Did he give you the key, Dion?' I asked him directly.

The kid shook his head.

'He doesn't have it,' Ivy said. 'He's too bad a liar to hide this from us, in my professional estimation.'

'What you should be doing,' Dion said, digging back into his burrito, 'is looking for some crazy device or something.'

'Device?'

'Sure,' Dion said. 'He'd have built something to hide it, you know? All that maker stuff, you know? He was always gluing LED lights to things and making his own name badges and things. I'll bet he hid it like that. You pick up a potato, and it knocks over a penny, and a hundred geese fly into the air, and the key drops on your head. Something like that.'

I looked at my aspects. They seemed skeptical, but maybe there was something to this. Not a device like Dion described, but a process. What if Panos had set up some sort of fail-safe that would reveal the truth if he died – but it hadn't been tripped for some reason.

I forced myself to eat a bit of omelet, just to be able to tell Wilson I'd done so when he inevitably asked. Unfortunately, my phone still hadn't beeped by the time we finished. I stalled as best I could, but eventually felt it would look suspicious to Zen if we stayed any longer.

I led the way back out to the SUV, and held open the side door for my aspects before rounding to the driver's seat. I'd just settled in, planning my next move, when I felt the cold metal of a gun barrel press against the back of my neck.

18

Dion climbed into the passenger seat, oblivious. He looked at me, then froze, going all white. I glanced at the rearview mirror and caught a glimpse of Zen squatting behind my seat, gun pressed against my head.

Damn. So she hadn't been as willing to wait as I'd hoped. My phone hung in my pocket like a dead weight. What was taking Wilson so long?

'Join me in the back, if you would please, Mister Leeds,' Zen said softly. 'Young Maheras, remain in place. I assume that I needn't warn you how willing I am to resort to violence?'

Sweating, I noticed J.C. in the rearview mirror, his face red. He'd been sitting in the seat that Zen now squatted before, but hadn't seen her until now. Twice she'd gotten the drop on us, and J.C. hadn't been able to do a thing. Her skill at this was far better than my own.

J.C. took out his gun, for all the good it would do, and nodded for me to obey Zen. Getting into the back would put me into a better position to engage her.

She moved to the far back seat – scrunching Ivy and Audrey to the sides – as I moved, her gun on me at all times.

'Your weapon,' she said.

I removed it, just as I had in the alley, and placed it before me on the floor. Why was I even carrying the blasted thing?

'Phone next.'

I passed it over.

'Good job on finding the bug,' she noted to me. 'We will discuss the matter further, Mister Leeds, as we go for a stroll together. Young Maheras, you are not involved in this. Move to the driver's seat of the car. Once we are out, you are to leave. I don't care what you do – go to the police, if you wish – but stay away. I don't like killing people I haven't been hired to hit. It's bad business to … give away too many freebies.'

Dion was all too quick to move, scrambling into the driver's seat, where I'd left the keys.

'This is good,' J.C. said softly. 'She's letting the boy go and is moving us out into the open.' He scrunched up his face. 'I can't figure out why she'd do either one, but I think it indicates that her superiors have demanded she not actually kill anyone.'

I nodded, sweat trickling down the back of my neck. Zen waved with her gun and I opened the side door, letting my aspects file out, J.C first, then Ivy, then Tobias. Audrey rested a hand on my arm encouragingly and I nodded, then moved to climb out before her.

Zen snapped forward, grabbing me by the shoulder and throwing me back. She snatched the door and slammed it closed.

'Maheras,' she said, turning the gun on him. 'Drive. *Now.*'

'But –'

'Go or you're a dead man!'

The kid floored it, running over a parking lot divider. I lay stunned against the side of the car, blinking, tracking what had happened. Zen …

My aspects!

I cried out, turning and pressing my face against the window. Ivy and Tobias stood out in the parking lot, looking baffled. Zen instructed Dion to pull out of the parking lot onto the street, and then told him to continue at a normal speed – no trying to get picked up by cops, please.

I barely listened. She'd lured my aspects out, then isolated me from them. Only Audrey was left, and that was by a fluke. Another moment, and she'd have been gone too. I turned, stunned, to look at Zen, who had settled into the seat by the now-closed door, her gun held on me.

'I do my research,' she said. 'As a side note, the amount that has been written about you in psychological journals was *quite* useful, Mister Leeds.'

Audrey sank down onto the floor between us, wrapping her hands around her knees, whimpering. She was all I had, for now, and –

Wait.

J.C. I hadn't seen J.C. out the window. I turned, searching, and there he was! Charging along the sidewalk at a full run, gun in one hand, look of determination on his face. He kept pace with us, barely.

Bless you, I thought toward him. He'd reacted when the other two were caught flat-footed. He dodged around some people on the sidewalk and leaped a bench in an almost superhuman move.

Audrey perked up, looking out the window. 'Wow,' she whispered. 'How is he *doing* that?'

The car was moving at around forty miles an hour. Suddenly, I couldn't pretend any longer. J.C. ran out of breath, lurched to a stop on the sidewalk, his face flushed. He collapsed, exhausted from a run he shouldn't have been able to manage.

The illusion. I *had* to keep the illusion. Audrey looked at me, then seemed to shrink upon herself, realizing what she'd done. It wasn't her fault, though. I'd have eventually noticed how fast we were going.

'You,' Zen said to me, 'are a very dangerous man.'

'I'm not the one holding the gun,' I said, turning to face her. How was I going to do this without Ivy and Tobias to help me interact? Without J.C. to pull me out of a deadly situation?

'Yes, but I can only kill the occasional individual,' Zen said. 'You bring down companies, destroy hundreds of lives. My employers are … concerned about what you've done.'

'And they think having you grab me is going to help?' I asked. 'I won't find Panos's key for you at gunpoint, Zen.'

'They're not worried about the body anymore,' she said, and sounded faintly troubled. 'You've toppled their fortunes and sent the government after them. They don't want to be associated with this hunt any longer. They just want … loose threads to be pulled out and disposed of.'

Great. My plan was working.

Too well.

I tried to come up with something more to say, but Zen turned from me, giving Dion a series of driving instructions. I tried to get her talking again, but she refused, and

I wasn't about to try anything physical. Not without J.C. to give advice.

Maybe ... maybe the other aspects would find their way to wherever we were going. Given time, they probably would.

I wasn't sure how long that would take.

Audrey spent the ride seated in the middle of the floor between our two seats, arms wrapped around her legs. I wanted to talk to her, but didn't dare say anything with Zen watching. The assassin thought she'd isolated me without any aspects. If I let her know that one was still here, I would lose a big advantage.

Unfortunately, our drive took us to an area on the outskirts of the city. There were some new housing developments out here, as the city's creeping expansion slowly consumed the countryside, but there were also big patches of fields and trees waiting for condos and gas stations. Zen had us pull into one of these large wooded spots, and we drove on a dirt road up to a solitary house of the 'my fathers farmed this land for generations' variety.

This was far enough from neighbors that shouts would not be heard and gunshots would be attributed to the removal of vermin. Not good. Zen marched Dion and me to a cellar door set in the ground and ordered us down the stairs. Inside, sacks slumped against the wall, spilling potatoes so old they'd probably witnessed the Civil War. A bare lightbulb glared where it hung from the center of the ceiling.

'I'm going to go report,' Zen told us, taking Dion's phone from him. 'Get comfortable. My expectation is that you're going to be living down here for a few weeks while things blow over for my employers.'

She walked up the steps and locked the cellar door.

19

Dion let out a deep breath and put his back to the cinder block wall, then slumped down to a sitting position. 'Weeks?' he asked. 'Trapped in here with you?'

I paused a moment before speaking. 'Yeah. That's going to suck, eh?'

Dion looked up at me, and I cursed myself for hesitating before giving my reply. The kid looked frazzled – he'd probably never been forced to drive at gunpoint before. First time is always the worst.

'You don't think we're going to be down here for weeks, do you?' Dion guessed.

'I ... No.'

'But she said –'

'They're trained to talk that way,' I said, fishing out Zen's bug from under my collar, then smashing it just in case. I walked around the chamber, looking for exits.

'Always tell your captives they have more time than they do; it makes them relax, sets them to planning, instead of trying to break out immediately. The last thing you want to do is make them desperate, since desperate people are unpredictable.'

The kid groaned softly. I probably shouldn't have explained that. I was feeling the lack of Ivy's presence. Even when she didn't guide me directly, having her around made me better at interacting with people.

'Don't worry,' I said, kneeling down to inspect a drain in the floor, 'we probably won't be in real danger unless Zen decides to take us individually into the woods "for questioning". That will mean she's been told to execute us.'

I prodded at the grate. Too small to crawl through, unfortunately, and it looked like it just ended in a small pit of rocks anyway. I moved on, expecting – despite myself – to hear commentary by my aspects analyzing our situation, telling me what to investigate, theorizing on how to get out.

Instead, all I heard was retching.

I spun on Dion, shocked to find him emptying his stomach onto the floor of the cellar. So much for the breakfast burrito he'd so stubbornly paid for. I waited until he was done, then walked over, taking an old towel off of a dusty table and draping it over the sick-up to smother the smell. I knelt down, resting my hand on the young man's shoulder.

He looked awful. Red eyes, pale skin, sweat on his brow.

How to interact? What did one say? 'I'm sorry.' It sounded lame, but it was all I could think of.

'She's going to kill us,' the youth whispered.

'She might try,' I said. 'But then again, she might not. Killing us is a big step, one her employers probably won't be willing to make.'

Of course, I *had* made them very desperate. And desperate people were … well, unpredictable.

I stood up, leaving the kid to his misery, and walked to Audrey. 'I need you to get us out of this,' I whispered to her.

'Me?' Audrey said.

'You're all I have.'

'Before this, I'd only been on a *single* mission!' she said. 'I don't know about guns, or fighting, or escaping.'

'You're an expert on cryptography.'

'Expert? You read *one* book on cryptography. Besides, how is cryptography going to help? Here, let me interpret the scratches on the walls. They say we're *bloody doomed!*'

Frustrated, I left her trembling with worry and forced myself to continue my inspection of the room.

No windows. Some sections of bare earth where the cinder-block wall had fallen in. I was able to dig at one, but heard the floor groaning above as I did. Not a good idea.

I tried the exit next, climbing the steps and shoving my shoulder at the doors to see how strong they were. They were tight, unfortunately, and there was no lock to pick – just a padlock on the outside that I couldn't reach. I might be able to find something to use as a ram and break us out, but that would certainly alert Zen. I could hear her through the floor above, talking. Sounded like a terse conversation over a cell phone, but I couldn't make out any specifics.

I went over the room again. Had I missed anything? I was sure I had, but what? Without my aspects, I didn't know what I knew. Being alone haunted me. As I passed Dion, I found the expressions on his face alien things, no more intelligible as emotions than lumps in mud. Did that expression mean happiness? Sorrow?

Stop, I told myself, sweating. *You're not that bad.* I was without Ivy, but that didn't suddenly make me unable to relate to members of my own species. Did it?

Dion was upset. That was obvious. He stared down at a few small slips of paper in his hands. More scriptures he'd found in his pockets from his mother.

'She just left the verse numbers,' he said, glancing at me, 'so I don't even know what the scriptures say. As if they'd be a help anyway. Bah!' He closed his fist, then threw the papers, wadded up. They burst apart from each other and fluttered down like confetti.

I stood there, feeling almost as sick as Dion looked. I needed to say something, connect with him somehow. I didn't know *why* I felt that, but I was suddenly desperate for it.

'Are you so frightened of death, Dion?' I asked. Probably the wrong words, but speaking was better than remaining silent.

'Why wouldn't I be?' Dion said. 'Death is the end. Nothing. All gone.' He looked at me, as if in challenge. When I didn't respond immediately, he continued. 'Not going to tell me everything will be all right? Mom always talks about how good people get rewarded, but Panos was as good a man as there was. He spent his life trying to cure disease! And look at him. Dead of a stupid *accident*.'

'Why,' I said, 'do you assume death is the end?'

'Because it *is*. Look, I don't want to listen to any religious –'

'I'm not going to preach at you,' I said. 'I'm an atheist too.'

The kid looked at me. 'You are?'

'Sure,' I said. 'Almost fifteen percent – though, admittedly, several of my pieces would argue that they are agnostic instead.'

'Fifteen percent? That doesn't count.'

'Oh? So you get to decide how my faith, or lack thereof, works? What "counts" and what doesn't?'

'No, but even if it did work that way – if someone could be *fifteen percent* atheist – the majority of you still believes.'

'Just like a minority of you probably still believes in God,' I said.

He looked at me, then blushed. I settled down beside him, opposite the place where he'd had his little accident.

'I can see why people want to believe,' Dion told me. 'I'm not just a petulant kid, like you think. I've wondered, I've asked. God doesn't make sense to me. But sometimes, looking at infinity and thinking of myself just ... not being here anymore, I understand why people would choose to believe.'

Ivy would want me to try to convert the boy, but she wasn't here. Instead, I asked a question. 'Do you think time is infinite, Dion?'

He shrugged.

'Come on,' I prodded. 'Give me an answer. You want comfort? I might have a solution for you – or at least my aspect Arnaud might. But first, is time infinite?'

'I don't think we know for certain,' Dion replied. 'But yeah, I'd guess that it is. Even after our universe ends, something *else* will happen. If not here, then in other dimensions. Other places. Other big bangs. Matter, space, it'll continue on without end.'

'So you're immortal.'

'My atoms, maybe,' he said. 'But that's not *me*. Don't give me any metaphysical bull–'

'No metaphysics,' I said, 'just a theory. If time is infinite, then anything that *can* happen *will* happen – and *has* happened. That means you've happened before, Dion. We all have. Even if there is no God – even supposing that there are no answers, no divinity out there – we're immortal.'

He frowned.

'Think about it,' I said. 'The universe rolled its cosmic dice and ended up with you – a semi-random collection of atoms, synapses, and chemicals. Together, those create your personality, memories, and very existence. But if time continues forever, eventually that random collection will happened again. It may take hundreds of trillions of years, but it *will* come again. You. With your memories, your personality. In the context of infinity, kid, we will keep living, over and over.'

'I … don't know how comforting that is, honestly. Even if it is true.'

'Really?' I asked. 'Because I think it's pretty amazing to consider. Anything that is *possible* is actually *reality*, given infinity. So, not only will you return, but your every iteration of possibility will play out. Sometimes you'll be rich. Sometimes you'll be poor. In fact, it's plausible that because of a brain defect, sometime in the future you'll have the memories you have now, even if in *that* future time you never lived those memories. So you'll be you again, completely, and not because of some mystical nonsense – but because of simple mathematics. Even the smallest chance multiplied by infinity is, itself, infinite.'

I stood back up, then squatted down, looking him in the eyes and resting my hand on his shoulder. 'Every variation of possibility, Dion. At some point, you – the same you, with the same thought processes – will be born to a wealthy family. Your parents will be killed, and you will decide to fight against injustice. It has happened. It will happen. You asked for comfort, Dion? Well, when the fear of death seizes you – when the dark thoughts come – you stare the darkness right back, and you tell it, "I will not listen to you, for I am *infinite Batmans*."'

The kid blinked at me. 'That … is the weirdest thing anyone has ever told me.'

I winked at him, then left him lost in thought and walked back to Audrey. I wasn't sure how much of that I actually believed, but it was what had come out. Honestly, I don't know that the universe could really handle everyone being infinite Batmans.

Perhaps the point of God was to prevent nonsense like that.

I took Audrey by the arm, speaking softly. 'Audrey, focus on me.'

She looked at me, blinking. She'd been crying.

'We're going to think, right now,' I told her. 'We're going to scrounge everything we know, and we're going to come up with a way out of this.'

'I can't –'

'You *can*. You're part of me. You're part of all of this; you can access my subconscious. You can *fix this*.'

She met my eyes, and some of my confidence seemed to transfer to her. She nodded sharply, and adopted a look of complete concentration. I smiled at her encouragingly.

The door to the building up above opened, then shut.

Come on, Audrey.

Zen's footsteps rounded the building, then she began working on the lock down into the cellar.

Come on …

Audrey snapped her head up and looked at me. 'I know where the body is.'

'The body?' I said. 'Audrey, we're supposed to be –'

'Zen's company doesn't have it,' Audrey said. 'I3 doesn't have it. The kid doesn't know anything. I *know where it is.*'

The door down into the cellar opened. Light flooded in, revealing Zen silhouetted above. 'Mister Leeds,' she said. 'I need you to come with me so I can question you alone. It will only take a short time.'

I grew very cold.

'Oh hell,' Audrey said, backing away from me. 'You need to do something! Don't let her kill you.'

I turned to face Zen – a woman dressed in chic clothing, like she was the CFO of a Manhattan publishing company, not a paid assassin. She walked down the steps, feigning nonchalance. That attitude, mixed with the tension of the call above, told me all I needed to know.

She was going to eliminate me.

'They're really willing to do this?' I asked her. 'It will leave questions. Problems.'

'I don't know what you're talking about.' She got out her gun.

'Do we have to play this game, Zen?' I replied, frantically searching for a way to stall. 'We both know what you're up to. You'll really follow through with orders that are so incompetent? It leaves you in danger. People *will* wonder where I've gone.'

'An equal number will be glad to have you out of their hair, I assume,' Zen said. She took out a suppressor, affixing it to her gun, all pretense gone now.

Audrey whimpered. To his credit, Dion stood up, unwilling to face death sitting down.

'You pushed them too hard, Mister Crazy,' Zen said. 'They have it in their heads that you're trying specifically to destroy them, and so they have responded as any bully does when shoved. They hit as hard as they can and hope it will solve the situation.' She raised the gun. 'As for me, I can take care of myself. But thank you for your concern.'

I stared down the barrel of that gun, sweating, panicking. No hope, no plan, no aspects …

But she didn't know that.

'They're around you,' I whispered.

Zen hesitated.

'Some people theorize,' I said, 'that the ones I see are ghosts. If you've read about me, then you'll know. I do things I shouldn't be able to. Know things I shouldn't know. Because I have help.'

'You're just a genius,' she said, but her eye twitched to the side. Yes, she'd read about me. Deeply, if she knew how to drive off without my aspects.

And nobody could dig into my world without coming away a little bit … touched.

'They've caught up to us,' I said. 'They stand on the steps behind you. Can you feel them there, Zen? Watching you? Hands at your neck? What will you do with them if you remove me? Will you live with my spirits stalking you for the rest of your life?'

She set her jaw, and seemed as if she was trying very, very hard not to look over her shoulder. Was this actually working?

Zen took a deep breath. 'They won't be the only spirits that haunt me, Leeds,' she whispered. 'If there is a hell, I earned my place in it long ago.'

'So you say,' I replied. 'Of course, what you really should be wondering is this: I'm a genius. I know things I shouldn't. So why have I placed us here, right now? Why is it that I *want* you right there?'

'I …' She held the gun on me. A cool breeze blew in down around her, rustling the lips of old potato sacks.

My cell phone chirped in her pocket.

Zen practically jumped to the ceiling. She cursed, sweating, and rested her hand on the pocket. She thrust the gun at me and fired. Wild. The support beam beside me popped with exploding bits of wood. Dion dove for cover.

Zen – eyes so wide, I could see the whites all around her pupils – held the gun in a trembling hand, focusing on me.

'Check the phone, Zen,' I said.

She didn't move.

No! It couldn't go this way. So close! She had to –

Another phone rang. Hers this time, I assumed, buzzing in her other pocket. Zen wavered. I met her stare. In that moment, one of the two of us was mad, insane, on the edge.

And it wasn't the crazy guy.

Her phone stopped ringing. A text followed. We waited, facing one another in the cold cellar until, at long last, Zen reached down and took out her phone. She stared at it for a few moments. Then she laughed a barking laugh. She backed up, placing a call, and had a whispered conversation.

Letting out what had to be the biggest breath of my life, I walked to Dion and helped him to his feet. He looked up at Zen, who laughed again, this time louder.

'What's going on?' Dion asked.

'We're safe,' I said. 'Isn't that right, Zen?'

She giggled wildly. Then she hung up and looked right at me. 'Whatever you say, sir.'

'… "Sir"?' Dion asked.

'Exeltec was on unstable footing,' I said. 'I released

rumors that it was involved in a federal investigation, and had Yol push all the right buttons economically.'

'To make them desperate?' Dion asked.

'To crash the company,' I said, walking back to Zen, passing a flummoxed Audrey. 'So I could afford to buy it. Yol was supposed to do that part, but only got halfway done. I had to have Wilson do the rest, calling the various Exeltec investors and buying them out.' I proffered my hand to Zen. She gave me my phone.

'So …' Dion said.

'So I now own a sixty percent stake in the company,' I said, checking the text from Wilson. 'And have voted myself president. That makes me Zen's boss.'

'Sir,' she said. She was doing a good job of regaining her composure, but I could see a wildness in the way her hands still trembled, the way she stood with her expression too stiff.

'Wait,' Dion said. 'You just defeated an assassin with a *hostile takeover?*'

'I use the cards dealt to me. Probably wasn't particularly hostile, though – I suspect that everyone involved was all too eager to jump ship.'

'You realize, of course,' Zen said smoothly, 'that I was never actually going to shoot you. I was just supposed to make you worried so you'd share information.'

'Of course.' That would be the official line, to protect her and Exeltec from attempted murder charges. My buyout agreement would include provisions to prevent me from taking action against them.

I pocketed my phone, took my gun back from Zen, and nodded to Audrey. 'Let's go collect that body.'

21

We found Mrs. Maheras in the garden still. She knelt there, planting, nurturing, tending.

I walked up, and from the way she glanced at me, I suspected she realized that her secret was out. Still, I knelt down beside her, then handed over a carton of half-grown flowers when she motioned toward them.

Sirens sounded in the distance.

'Was that necessary?' she asked, not looking up.

'Sorry,' I said. 'But yes.' I'd sent a text to Yol, knowing the feds would get it first. Behind me, Audrey, Tobias, Ivy, and a downcast J.C. stepped up to us. They cast shadows, to my eyes, in the fading light, and blocked my view of Dion standing just behind. We'd found them all walking along the road, miles from Zen's holding place, trying to reach me.

I was tired. Man, was I tired. Sometimes, in the heat of

it all, you can forget. But when the tension ends, it comes crashing down.

'I should have seen it,' Ivy said again, arms folded. 'I *should* have. Most Orthodox branches are pointedly against cremation. They see it as desecration of the body, which is to await resurrection.'

We had been so focused on the information in Panos's cells that we didn't stop to think there might be other reasons entirely that someone would want to take the corpse. Reasons so powerful that it would convince an otherwise law-abiding woman and her priest to pull a heist.

In a way, I was very impressed. 'You were a cleaning lady when you were younger,' I said. 'I should have asked Dion more about your life, your job. He mentioned hard labor, a life spent supporting him and his brother. I didn't ask what you'd done.'

She continued planting flowers upon her son's grave, hidden in the garden.

'You imitated the cleaning lady who worked at the morgue,' I said. 'You paid her off, I assume, and went in her place – after having the priest place tape on the door. It really was him, not an impostor. Together, you went to extremes to protect your son's corpse from cremation.'

'What gave me away?' Mrs. Maheras asked as the sirens drew closer.

'You followed the real cleaning lady's patterns exactly,' I said. 'Too exactly. You cleaned the bathroom, then signed your name on the sheet hanging on the door, to prove it had been done.'

'I practiced Lilia's signature exactly!' Mrs. Maheras said, looking at me for the first time.

'Yes,' I said, holding up one of the slips of paper with scriptures on them that she put in her son's pockets. 'But you wrote the cleaning time on that sheet as well, and you didn't practice imitating Lilia's *numbers*.'

'You have a very distinctive zero,' Audrey explained, looking supremely smug. Cryptography hadn't cracked this case after all. It had just required some good, old-fashioned handwriting analysis.

Mrs. Maheras sighed, then placed her spade into the dirt and bowed her head, offering a silent prayer. I bowed my head as well, as did Ivy and J.C. Tobias refrained.

'So you'll take him again,' Mrs. Maheras whispered, once she had finished. She looked at the ground before her, now planted with flowers and tomatoes.

'Yes,' I said, climbing to my feet and dusting off my knees. 'But at the very least, you're unlikely to be in too much trouble for what you did. The government doesn't recognize a body as property, so what you did wasn't actually theft.'

'A cold comfort,' she muttered. 'They'll still take him, and they'll burn him.'

'True,' I said idly. 'Of course, who knows what secrets your son had hidden in his body? He'd been splicing secret information into his very DNA, and he might have hidden all kinds of things in there. The right implication at the right time might prod the government into a very, *very* long search.'

She looked up at me.

'Scientists disagree on how many cells there are in the human body,' I explained. 'Somewhere in the trillions, easily. Perhaps many more than that. Could take decades upon decades to search them all, something I doubt the government will want to do. However, if they think there *might* be something important, they could likely set the body into storage just in case they need to do a thorough search at some point.

'It wouldn't be a proper burial, as you want – but it also wouldn't be cremation. I believe the church does make provisions for people donating organs to help others? Perhaps it's best to just consider it in that light.'

Mrs. Maheras seemed thoughtful. I left her then, and Dion stepped forward to comfort her. My suggestions did seem to have made a difference, which baffled me. I'd have rather seen a family member cremated than spend forever being frozen. However, as I reached the building and looked back, I found that Mrs. Maheras seemed to have perked up visibly.

'You were right,' I told Ivy.

'Have I ever *not* been right?'

'I don't know about that,' J.C. said. 'But you *do* make some really bad relationship choices sometimes.'

We all looked at him, and he blushed immediately.

'I was talking about her *dumping* me,' he protested. 'Not picking me in the first place!'

I smiled, leading the way into the kitchen. I was just glad to have them back. I walked down the little hallway lined with pictures, toward the front door. I'd want to meet the feds when they arrived.

Then I stopped. 'There's a bare patch on the wall. It looks so odd. Every surface, desk, and wall in this place is covered with kitsch. Except here.' I pointed at the pictures of the family, then two pictures of saints. Two spots, empty save for little nails. Ivy had said that Mrs. Maheras had probably taken down the picture of Panos's patron saint in preparation for his funeral.

'Ivy,' I said, 'would you say it's safe to assume that Panos knew if he died, this picture would be removed and placed with his corpse?'

We looked at each other. Then I reached up and pulled

on the nail. It resisted in an odd fashion. I yanked harder, and the nail came out – but had a knob and string tied around the back end.

Behind the wall, something clicked.

I looked at the aspects, suddenly worried, until the wall's nearby light switch – plate behind it and all – rotated forward like a hidden cup holder in a car's dashboard. The portion that had been hidden inside the wall had LED lights blinking on the sides.

'Well I'll be damned,' J.C. said. 'The kid was right.'

'Language,' Ivy mumbled, looking closely at the contraption.

'What happened to the future curses?' Audrey said. 'I kind of liked those.'

'I realized something,' J.C. said. 'I can't be an Inter-dimensional Time Ranger. Because if I am, that means all of *you* are too. And that's just a little too silly for me to accept.'

I reached into the holder that had come out and extracted a thumb drive. Written on it, with a label maker, were a few words.

'1 Kings 19:11–12,' I read.

'And He said,' Ivy quoted in a quiet voice, 'Go forth, and stand upon the mount before the Lord. And behold, the Lord passed by, and a great and strong wind rent the mountains and broke in pieces the rocks before the Lord, but the Lord was not in the wind; and after the wind an earthquake, but the Lord was not in the earthquake. And after the earthquake a fire, but the Lord was not in the fire; and after the fire a still small voice.'

I looked at my aspects as a fist pounded on the door. Then I pocketed the thumb drive and pushed the holder back into the wall before going to meet with the feds.

EPILOGUE

Four days later, I stood alone in the White Room. Tobias had covered over the hole in the ceiling, as he'd promised. The place was refreshingly blank.

Was this what I would be, without my aspects? Blank? I'd certainly felt that way while being held by Zen. I'd barely been able to do anything to save myself. No plans, no escaping. Just some stalling. Ivy had sometimes wondered if I was growing good enough on my own that I eventually wouldn't need her or the others any longer.

From what had happened to me when I'd lost them, I figured that day – if it ever came – was a long, long way off.

The door cracked open. Audrey slipped in, wearing a blue one-piece swimsuit. She trotted up to me and delivered a sheet of paper. 'Have to go catch a pool party. But I did finish solving this. Wasn't too hard, once we had the key.'

On the thumb drive, we'd found two things. The first was the anticipated key to unlocking the data on Panos's body. The body had been seized by the government, and I'd convinced them to put it on ice for the foreseeable future. After all, there might be very, very important data on it, and someday the key might turn up.

Yol had offered me an exorbitant amount to track down the key. I'd refused, though I had forced him to buy Exeltec from me for another exorbitant sum, so I came away from this in a good enough position.

The CDC failed to find evidence that Panos had released any kind of pathogen, and eventually determined that the note on Panos's computer had been an idle threat, meant to send I3 into a panic. Earlier that morning, Dion had sent me a thank-you note from him and his mother for stopping the government from burning the body. I hadn't yet told them I'd stolen this thumb drive.

It contained the key, and a ... second file. A small text document, also encrypted. We'd stared at it for a time before realizing that the key had been printed on the outside of the thumb drive itself. Chapter nineteen of First Kings. Any string of letters or numbers, or mixture of the two, can be the passphrase for a private-key cryptogram – though using a known text, like Bible verses, wasn't a particularly secure option.

Audrey went out, but left the door cracked open. I could see Tobias outside, leaning against the wall, arms folded, wearing his characteristic loose business suit, no tie.

I raised the sheet of paper, reading the simple note Panos had left.

I guess I'm dead.

I shouldn't be surprised, but I didn't think they'd ever actually go through with it. My own friends, you know?

He'd gotten that wrong. So far as I, or anyone else could determine, his fall really had been an accident.

Did you know every person is a walking jungle of bacteria? We're each a little biome, all to ourselves. I've made an alteration. It's called Staphylococcus epidermidis. A strain of bacteria we all carry. It's harmless, for the most part.

My changes aren't big. Just an addition. Several megs of data, spliced into the DNA. I3 was watching me, but I learned to do my work even when supervised. They watched what I posted, though, so I decided to use their tools against them. I put the information into the bacteria of my own skin and shook hands with them all. I'll bet you can find strains of my altered bacteria all across the world by now.

It won't do anything harmful. But if you've found this, you have the key to decoding what I've hidden. You make the call, Dion. I leave it in your hands. Release the key on this thumb drive, and everyone will know what I've studied. They'll have the answers to what I3 is doing, and everyone will be on an even playing field.

I studied the paper for a time, then quietly folded it and slipped it into my back pocket. I walked to the door.

'Are you going to do it?' Tobias asked as I passed him. 'Let it out?'

I pulled out the flash drive and held it up. 'Didn't Dion talk about about starting a new company with his brother? Curing disease? Doing good each day?'

'Something like that,' Tobias said.

I tossed the drive up into the air, then caught it. 'We'll set this aside, to be mailed to him on the day he graduates. Maybe that dream of his isn't as dead as he thinks. At the very least, we should honor his brother's wishes.' I hesitated. 'But we'll want to see if we can get the data ourselves first and check out how dangerous it might be.'

As my aspects had guessed, my contacts among the feds said the cancer scare had been a fake on Yol's part, an attempt to make my task urgent. But we had no idea what Panos had really been working on. Somehow, he'd hidden that even from the people at I3.

'Technically,' Tobias said, 'that information is owned by Yol.'

'Technically,' I said, pocketing the flash drive again, 'it's owned by *me* as well, since I'm part owner of the company. We'll just call this my part.'

I passed him, heading to the stairs. 'The funny thing is,' I said, hand on the banister, 'we spent this entire time searching for a corpse – but the information wasn't just there. It was on every person we met.'

'There's no way we could have known,' Tobias said.

'Of course there was,' I said. 'Panos warned us. That day we studied I3 – it was proclaimed right there, on one of the slogans he'd printed and hung on his wall.'

Tobias looked at me, quizzical.

'Information,' I said, wiggling my fingers – and the bacteria that held Panos's data, 'for every body.'

I smiled, and left Tobias chuckling as I went searching for something to eat.

ACKNOWLEDGMENTS

First off, I'd like to thank Moshe Feder, who edited this book for me, along with the Inscrutable Peter Ahlstrom, who did some serious bonus editing. Thanks to Isaäc Stewart and Kara Stewart for their assistant-fu on this and many other projects. Howard Tayler also helped me brainstorm at lunch one day, and gets a writer high-five for his help.

My beta readers on this volume were: Mi'chelle Walker, Josh Walker, Kalyani Poluri, Rahul Pantula, Kaylynn ZoBell, Peter & Karen Ahlstrom, Ben & Danielle Olsen, Darci & Eric James Stone, Alan Layton, Emily Sanderson, and Kathleen Dorsey Sanderson.

At Subterranean, the original publisher, I'd like to thank Yanni Kuznia, Bill Schafer, Morgan Schlicker, and Gail Cross. Isaac Stewart's great new cover design graces this edition.

As always, many thanks to my wonderful family, including my three very excited – and very busy – little boys.

Brandon Sanderson